# Against All Odds

# Against All Odds

Nicky J. Mason

Troubador Publishing Ltd
Unit E2 Airfield Business Park,
Harrison Road, Market Harborough,
Leicestershire. LE16 7UL
Tel: 0116 2792299
Email: books@troubador.co.uk
Web: www.troubador.co.uk

ISBN 978 1805142 768

British Library Cataloguing in Publication Data.
A catalogue record for this book is available from the British Library.

Typeset in 11pt Minion Pro by Troubador Publishing Ltd, Leicester, UK

To my Mason crew, for your continued love and support.

# One

"Look at the state of our Jamie here, Mum." Troy laughed, sinking lower into the cushions. Dawn stretched her feet out on the chaise longue. She took the photo from him and laughed. Her cute little girl, dressed as Hannah Montana, with squares of glitter paper glued to her Asda dress and cowgirl stickers on her wellington boots.

"She's certainly got more stylish with age." Dawn handed the picture back and crossed her legs.

He gave the picture one more glance, then dropped it with a roll of the eyes. "I'd have thought you, of all people, would have told her."

She side-eyed him. "Have you ever tried to tell a young girl what to wear?" She grimaced. Dawn knew that her daughter would never have listened to her advice, and besides, wasn't that what youth was all about? Expressing your individuality in your own way. She'd have hated herself for being a creative blocker.

He reached for another handful of photos. "Why don't you let me put all of these on a memory stick for you?" he asked, waving them in the air.

"No. I like having memories I can hold onto. Plus, things get forgotten about in outer space."

"Outer space?" He laughed.

"You know what I mean," she sighed.

"I think you mean cyberspace, but we could make you a nice folder on your desktop."

She shrugged it off. He skimmed through the pile in his hands, a sentimental glisten in his eyes.

"Oooh, this was in Milan when they went Versace mad," he gasped.

She glanced over. "That wasn't too long after Gianni's death, either. I think his sister wanted to make it spectacular." She picked up a pile herself.

There was a photo of the Paris skyline at night. She had taken it from the Eiffel Tower. It wasn't even from that night, twenty-two years ago. Camera phones weren't a thing then, and she hadn't been the type to carry a camera. The picture was from a more recent visit; when she had returned. Even so, her muscles tightened, her pulse quickened, and she longed to be there, standing on the Eiffel Tower, just so that she could somehow be closer to the memory.

Troy glanced over at her. "What's up with your mug?" he grinned.

She brought herself back to the present moment with a blink of the eyes. "Nothing," she said, slapping a smile on her face. "Anyway, you only liked that Milan show for those Asian boys."

He turned to her then, his eyes widening, his mouth opening. "What?" he gasped.

"Don't deny it. You thought they looked so cool in their Perspex coats and loafers with high socks."

He put his hand on his chest, visibly releasing air from his lungs. "God, I wondered what you meant. Yes, yes, the show was impressive. I also loved the leopard skin. Remember the leopard skin, Mum?"

He sounded a little breathless, she noted.

"I remember those trousers." She laughed. "Wait a minute, you had the orange jacket too, didn't you? Are there any photos in here of you in the orange jacket?"

"Hopefully not." He muttered.

She turned and watched as he rifled through the pile, a smile on his face. "This is nice," she said.

"What is?"

"Us. Spending time together, not shouting at each other."

"Urh. Don't start getting all sentimental on me."

"I'm serious. It's been a long time coming."

He looked at her for a moment. "Fancy a cuppa, Mum?" he asked, rising from his seat.

"I'll make it. You're my guest."

"It's fine, I'll get it."

He went to the kitchen. She heard the kettle flick on, the tinker of cups. She picked the Paris photo back up. She had returned to Paris alone almost a decade after the time she'd spent there. She'd toured the Eiffel Tower, the Arc de Triomphe. Drank coffee at one of the quaint outdoor café tables. Even sat on the bridge of the river Seine with a cheese and ham baguette. But none of it had felt the same. The clouds were dull; the people seemed grumpy and irritated. Some of the boutiques had been closed down. The cafés and wine bars, which had previously made her feel so sophisticated and hip, seemed then to be full of teenagers who didn't want to share their space with a has-been. When she meandered the old, cobbled roads, instead of feeling the romance in the tiny streets and old buildings, she'd seen decaying brickwork and tight roads full of angry drivers. Instead of champagne fountains, flashing camera lights and Louis Vuitton designs, she saw Costa Coffee and overspilling bins that smelt like gone-off fish.

It was as though Paris had lost its va-va-voom.

"Have you got any sweetener?" Troy called through.

Dawn got up from the comfy sofa. She swept her hand down her Dior A-line skirt and meandered into the kitchen. Troy was leaning over the steaming mugs, texting. There was a half-bitten cookie sat on the work surface, with crumbs around it. She pulled the sweeteners from the cupboard and passed them to him. He slipped his phone into his back jean pocket and popped several sweeteners into one of the mugs.

"I made some cookies; would you like one?" she asked with a smirk.

He turned, distracted. "I already…" He grinned. She pursed her lips, smiling with her eyes.

"Seen your dad and Leslie lately?" she asked.

"We went for Sunday lunch a couple of weeks ago."

"How are they?"

"They're well." He sighed, dipping a teaspoon into the mugs. "They seem happy."

"You don't need to be sad about that," she said, touching his arm. "It's a good thing, Troy."

"I know, but…" He paused and turned to her. "Do you think you'll ever meet anyone else, um?"

She leant back on the counter and folded her arms. "I'm sixty bloody two. Where am I going to meet someone?"

"I don't know, the supermarket? That weird rambling group you're a part of?"

"The thing is, Troy, after being with someone for twenty years, you soon realise what you don't want from a relationship."

"You weren't sixty-two when you broke up. It's been so long."

"I'm happy as I am. I don't need anyone to clean up after. I get to choose what's on TV, go out when I want to go out, and get back when I get back. I even get to have a lie-in without someone judging me."

He dropped the saturated tea bags into the bin and passed her the mug. "I suppose it has its advantages. But don't you get lonely?"

"Nah, I used to, when you kids first left home. Now I'm quite happy pottering about the house. Spending time with you all at my own leisure. Plus, Matt showed me how to use the YouTube. So, I can watch years of fashion week now whilst I bake or do jigsaws."

He started laughing.

"What's funny?"

"*The YouTube*? You crack me up."

"Last week I watched *Breakfast at Tiffany's* on Netflix."

"Not the Netflix then?" He sniggered.

"Huh?"

"Ah, nothing. Good. Good for you," he said, blowing on his tea.

"What about you?" she asked.

"I have Netflix." He replied, dipping the tiny piece of cookie into his tea, and watching it droop.

"No, I mean, you're living alone. And *you're* still young."

His face went blank then, as though he was pondering his response.

"Aren't you?" she asked.

"What, young? Not really, Mum. I'm twenty-nine now, you know."

She shook her head. "You're evading my question. You always do that."

"Oh, here we go again. Can't you go a single day without moaning?"

His phone rang, and he raised his eyebrows at her as he whipped it from his pocket.

"Hello?"

He leant against the counter, with his phone to his ear, tapping his toe on the ground. He sucked in his cheeks in concentration. And within seconds, he was pulling on his shoes and had reached for the door.

"Sorry, Mum, got to see a client," he called back as he raced away.

Dawn walked over to the kitchen window. Troy's full cup of tea sat steaming on the counter. *Was it a client or just an excuse to escape? Had she pushed too hard?*

She wrapped her thin, weathered hands around her mug of tea. Troy's Audi TT pulled off the drive. The rain pelted the streets alongside his car roof, bringing with it memories, evoked by those photographs. She reflected on that previous visit to Paris. Remembering the week she'd spent there. It still surprised her that she'd been fortunate enough to experience so many wonderful things in her life. And yet, that one week had ever since remained a comfort to her whenever that familiar longing crept over her.

Troy's car was long gone. Even so, she stared out at the rain with a blur in her eyes. A family down the road ran towards their house, giggling under the icy water that soaked them through. Dawn smiled to herself. She was happy in Great Bowden, where children played out on the street and the retirees got together, rambling amongst nature. But thinking about Paris always brought with it a mixture of emotions and regret. She had never told anyone about that week, although sometimes tempted. But then, she'd wondered how to start, and the moment always passed before she got the chance. Until she'd felt glad. It was a piece of her that nobody could judge or be opinionated about. It was a piece of her they may never know. Although…

The phone rang, breaking her from her thoughts.

"Troy came round last night," Jamie said.

"Oh?" she enquired.

"It was weird, Mum. He sat playing with Mia and Jake for ages. He even gave Mark some legal advice about a customer at work."

"Well, isn't that funny? He has also been sitting with me all afternoon. We were looking through photos, we were reminiscing."

Jamie huffed down the phone. "Is he there now?" she whispered.

"No, he got a fake call and had to rush off."

Jamie laughed. "Mum, he's been so against the family for so long. You don't think he's dying, do you?"

"No, I don't think he's dying, Jamie. I suspect he's met someone. Maybe he's getting ready to tell us he's in love."

"What makes you think that?"

"Just something he said tonight, something about me being alone. Also, when I mentioned his living situation, he was evasive. But not in the way he usually is."

"I'd still go with the dying thing. But you're right, he seems strangely happy."

"Well, whatever it is, I don't think it's bad news. When I saw him tonight, he was like the old Troy. He was chatty and funny and calm. Not as irritable."

"I'm gonna call Matt. Maybe Troy visited him and Joanne, too."

Dawn washed her mug at the kitchen sink, watching through the window as the rain calmed to a rhythmic tap. She walked to the back room and stacked the photos away, glancing through them as she did. She looked up with a contented sigh and caught her own reflection in the mirror; she saw a woman twice the age of the woman she felt. The face she saw in front of her was all skin and bone. She touched the scar on her right eyebrow from a stumble off a stage. The wrinkles by her eyes were from laughter and the pain of loss was below the eyeline. Her face was proof of a full life. She wondered how she could appreciate it, how she could keep a hold of the memories and the moments. Dawn wondered if sharing her secret would help her son to finally open up.

She stacked away the photos into the huge cardboard box. She'd kept the box with all the other memorabilia and junk in her old studio. These days, she barely even opened the door. She thought about stripping it out and creating an extra bedroom, something for the grandkids, but hadn't yet been able to bring herself to do it.

Carefully, she placed the photos back into the box. In the bottom lay a mound of newspaper articles and magazine clippings. Memories she hadn't dared to face for as many years as they had been there. She stared at them for a long moment, when the corner of the letter caught her eye.

Carefully, she pulled it from under the pile and unfolded it. It was yellow and tattered, and stuck together as she prized it apart.

*Dawn,*

*I am about to do it.*

*I hope you still want this. I hope you haven't got home from Paris and suddenly thought that it seems so silly and unrealistic. Like a teenage holiday romance that will wilt and die into a distant memory. I just don't think I could bear the thought of us dying like that. Everything in London suddenly seems so dull and lifeless without you here. If I stay here without you, I might just suffocate.*

*It's like I've been living in a bubble and the moment I met you, my entire world changed. Like a parallel universe where everything is brighter. I know it's all so sudden and even to me; I feel a bit vulnerable. But I've stuck to the rules for so long now and look where that's got me. I am here and willing to be vulnerable, for once in my life, for the sake of us.*

*Wish me luck and please, please, wait for me. xxx*

She folded the yellowing letter between her fingers. She sniffed it, as she remembered the joy in that moment. Knowing that they would be together again. Remembering how it had felt to fall so completely, as though it were yesterday. And so, she decided that on Saturday afternoon, after she'd been to visit her grandkids, she was going to get a nice bottle of chardonnay. She would take it, with the letter and the articles, over to Troy's apartment. And she was going to tell him everything.

# Two

Just after 2pm on Saturday, the city of Leicester was queuing in traffic. Toxic fumes, wafts of a chemically induced marijuana and the occasional *thump*, *thump*, *thump* of dull, heavy rap music flowed through the air. A couple wearing beanie hats with tattoos that spread all the way up their necks kissed before inhaling and blowing out clouds of vape smoke. People on delivery bikes weaved in and out of cars and up the curbs at dangerous speeds.

Troy's apartment, directly in the centre, whilst outside was busy and polluted, inside it was a different story. He had decorated the apartment in white gloss; it was squeaky clean and had the aroma of peonies and lemongrass. As Dawn followed her son through the hallway, she spotted a magnificent Bière Jules piece of art on his wall. A nineteenth-century tailor marvelling at his creation. She stopped and stared, lost in its magnificence. Tears filled her eyes, and she realised it wasn't the picture but the fact that he was just like her. They had so much in common and yet had wasted so much time being stubborn and afraid with each other. He was too scared that she would see him differently; she was too scared of losing him.

On a huge, dark wooden console table below was a bowl of pot-pourri, and a photo of Troy and a bearded, laughing man with a kind face. The man was wearing a costume that looked like a fried egg and he had one leg in the air. Troy was wearing what looked like a strip of bacon, and they both had on giant sized, bright yellow, plastic glasses, as they laughed at one another. They were standing in front of a large, wooden, mossy door all decorated in Halloween banners with a clown mask that hung on a hook behind them.

She smiled and slipped off her pumps before following the sound of Troy's voice, her feet creaking the original wooden panel floors.

He was talking to someone, and she trod lighter to listen.

"We'll sit in the kitchen. Will you still be able to concentrate?"

"Of course. I'm fine," replied the muffled male voice, and she felt her hopes rise. *Was this a boyfriend? Still in the house?*

"So, just stay there. We shouldn't be too long. Okay?"

"Fine. But you know this is ridiculous, don't you, Troy? It's like you're ashamed of me or something," came the muffled voice.

"You know I'm not ashamed of you."

"Do I? How would I know that, Troy?"

"Stop raising your voice. My mother is in there."

"Fine, go. Leave me here alone. I'll be okay."

"Oh, don't be ridiculous. You're working anyway."

“Even if I wasn’t, I’d have to be locked out like a dog.”

“Get over it,” he snapped.

He came around the kitchen counter and hastily began pouring Doritos into a bowl, along with some feta, olives and a guac dip into several other smaller pots. She saw him scowl at the door, heard it shut. He placed the bowls onto a small, round table. She handed him the bottle of wine.

“Sorry about that,” he said, finally looking at her. “I have a friend living here. He works from home.”

“None of my business,” she said.

She placed her coat onto the back of the chair.

“So, what’s up?” he asked.

“I wanted to speak with you,” she said.

She thought how stylish he looked, in a simple, long-sleeved white t-shirt and black skinny jeans with leather boots. He squinted at her, raising one neatly shaped eyebrow.

“So, you said. But what is this about, Mother?” he asked.

She sat down at the table, looking around. There were no signs of another person living there. But there were no signs of Troy living there, either. The house was spotless. The only out of place item was a strange green bottle with a handle and spout on the windowsill beside a fake eucalyptus.

She turned to him, distracted. “Troy? Is that a bong?”

Troy’s head whipped round.

“For goodness’ sake. It’s not mine, it’s my friend’s, the one who’s living here. Please don’t make a big deal out of it.”

He picked it up.

"So, you're a stoner now, are you?"

"No, I'm not a bloody stoner. I don't like the stuff; it makes me feel weird."

He walked out of the room with the bottle in his hand. He closed the door tight. She heard strained mutters. He walked back in with pursed lips and picked up the abandoned wine glasses.

He sat down in the chair across from her. She watched as he poured them both a glass of wine. She popped an olive into her mouth, felt it squidge between her teeth.

"Everything okay?"

He rolled his eyes. "Yes."

"Okay." She knew not to push the subject any further.

She watched as he closed his eyes and took in a deep breath and brightened.

"Let's try again, shall we? Actually, don't tell me," he said, sitting up and wrapping his ankles around the legs of his chair. "I'll guess. Ready?"

She looked back at him, her mouth poised in a half chew.

"You've met a man, and he's in a biker crew. But you've since found out that they also deal in drugs and guns. And they kill people who get in their way. And he is basically their, like, pack leader?"

She glared at him. "This is not bloody *Sons of Anarchy*, Troy."

"Sons of what?" he replied with a smirk. "You should never have got Netflix." He smiled. "Okay, if it's not that, next guess then. You're... having a boob job? No, no. Your marrow won top prize in a competition? Hmm, too obscure. You're taking up knitting?"

He looked at her lost expression. "Okay, last one, last one, I've got it now. You're getting back together with Dad?" He laughed into his wine glass.

She looked up at him and she laughed too.

"Let's not get carried away, Troy," she said, grabbing her own wine and taking a long pull. "Enough of the guessing. But if it's okay, I would like to tell you a story of what happened in my life when you were just a boy."

His forehead creased in concern. "Alright, I'm listening."

# Three

Paris 2001

Jane George zipped up her Prada duffle bag. She sat on the edge of the hotel room bed and stared at the cream swirls of the hotel carpet. She rolled her forefingers over the pressure points behind her eyes, then picked up the phone off the floor and opened it.

She typed: *Fashion week is over! I'm coming home. :)*

The reply was instant.

James: *Wait, already? I'm off to Japan tomorrow for a conference.*

Jane: *So, I won't see you?*

James: *No. What a shame. Seems like forever since I last saw you.*

She typed: *That's because it is. You really have to go tomorrow? On my fortieth birthday?*

She deleted the message and dropped the phone onto the bed. *Had he forgotten?*

It had been a month since she'd seen her husband. Longer since they'd been on an actual date, and she couldn't remember the last time they'd had sex. Although she didn't particularly want sex with anyone. She had never seen what all the fuss was about.

She chewed her bottom lip, standing and stretching out. Her bags were stacked by the doorway, ready to go home – to an empty house. She slipped on her shoes, checked her face in the mirror, and ran a hand over a perfectly arched eyebrow.

There was a soft tap at the door. She opened it.

"Bella," she cried, kissing the girl on both cheeks.

Bella Bernstein stood in front of her, one leg bent behind her.

"Hello, Jane." Bella had a Yugoslavian accent, and Jane suspected Bella not to be her real name. She was a petite 20-year-old girl, with sleek pulled back hair and cat-like eyes. She was a stunner alright; Jane could see why she was getting a load of hype.

"How are ya girl? I ain't seen you since, what, Los Angeles? Lavada conference halls?" Jane heard her own response, and suddenly felt conscious of her south-London accent. She always did around other models.

"That's right, it's been manic. I don't even know where the year has gone. I've been doing three shows a day lately."

"Oh god, I remember those days. Bless you."

"I rented a house eighteen months ago. I think I've spent one night in it."

"You must be mad. Why rent at all? I used to hotel hop. Much cheaper, and nothing to clean."

"For entertaining, of course. It's in central London, it's exquisite."

"I'm sure it is. So, what brings you here anyway?"

"Marilyn wants to see you. She's in the penthouse," she said.

Jane stared at her, blank faced. "She wants to see me. Why?"

"I don't know. But I don't think it's a bad thing. She has journos in there with her, too."

"Does she?"

"Yep. You just turned forty, didn't you? Is that why you're worried?"

"I'm forty tomorrow. And Marilyn might be the organiser of a lot of the events, but she don't own my career. I work for me."

"Oh, of course you do. I know that. You don't need her with a name like yours."

"Yeah, well."

Jane glared at Bella. The girl had her entire career ahead of her; she was in the beginning stages of a lot of challenging work and not much of a life.

"So, are you going out celebrating on the Parisian town tomorrow evening?" Bella asked.

"Nope."

"I don't blame you. I wouldn't celebrate turning forty either." She stood for a moment, as though deep in thought.

"What?" asked Jane.

"It's just, I've never actually known a model as old as you. Aside from your mum, of course, but I never met her, I just envied her pictures from afar."

"Thanks," she said sarcastically.

"I didn't mean to offend you. I think it's amazing that you haven't been sent to the retirement home yet."

"Again. Thanks."

Bella sighed.

"Sorry."

"Forget it. Honestly," she said, with a cool flap of the hand. She smiled on a deep inhale, meeting Bella's eyes. She genuinely didn't care if people thought she was too old for modelling, she knew what the industry was like, and she was ready to move on from it all. The thought gave her a moment of clarity, like something had been lifted… she didn't want to be a model anymore. Hairspray and perfume had been the air she breathed; she had grown up with the models of the eighties. In changing rooms, they would read her stories and help with her homework. She had no idea how to be without it, but she was willing to give it a try.

"I bet you could get by on your mum's name alone."

"I wouldn't want to."

"You've got to use what you can in this world, Jane."

"I hate the idea of needing to use her name, I want to do something different."

"Sounds like hard work to me."

"Bring it on, I say."

"Why bother at your age?"

Jane's mouth flopped open. "I'm forty. Not bloody eighty," she exclaimed.

"I'm not saying you're old in normal terms, but in this world." She blew air through her closed lips. "You never wanted to be a homemaker? Or have kids?"

"Nah."

The idea of spending every day at home waiting for James sounded like her idea of hell. Bella shrugged her shoulders and pursed her lips.

"I'd better go find that man of mine. No doubt he will be somewhere drinking champagne or flirting with someone."

Jane laughed as Bella turned to leave.

"You go and see her majesty, see what she wants. Maybe she has a new opportunity for you," she said, turning in the direction of the corridor.

Jane's stomach sank. What if Marilyn did have a new opportunity for her? Would she take it? Jane craved something else. Something that even she hadn't yet worked out, and she hoped, given time, that she would work it out whatever it was that had left this gaping hole inside of her.

Jane watched her press the button on the lift.

"Erm, Bella?" she called after her, pressing her shoulder into the doorframe.

Bella paused for a moment, turning only her ear back in Jane's direction.

"Try not to lose sight of yourself. It may not seem it now, but there's more to life than modelling."

Bella tilted her head back and laughed. "Pah, like that's even an option. I've got some big shoes to try and fill," she called back.

The lift pinged, and the doors opened. Bella got onto the lift; Jane walked into her room.

"Oh, and Jane George?" she called back, mimicking Jane's tone.

Jane stopped with the door in her hand, she peeked around.

"Try not to get fat in retirement. You never know when you will be photographed."

Jane's lips curved upward as she headed back inside and closed the door.

# Four

"So, you're telling me a story about a retiring model?" Troy asked, looking at his mother like she'd gone insane.

"I'll get to the point shortly, have patience," she said, crossing her legs and hugging her knee.

A face appeared around the kitchen door and momentarily startled Dawn. That was, until she recognised the man from the picture in the hall.

"You're not talking about *the* Jane George, are you?" he asked. "The model of the noughties who created that big buzz about beauty of all shapes and ages?"

"Out," demanded Troy.

"What?" The man looked hurt.

"Mitch, I said you could stay home on the condition that you were not to come in here."

"I know and I'm sorry, but you're talking about Jane George. How can I not come in?"

"Easy. Do as I ask."

"Is this the stoner?" Dawn asked, raising one eyebrow.

Troy smirked and turned to meet Mitch's eye. "Yeah, this is the stoner, Mum."

"He's joking, Mrs Cross. I'm not a stoner. Not really. I smoke occasionally, to relax."

Troy turned and widened his eyes at Mitch.

"It's Miss Lewis, better yet, Dawn. And relax, Troy. I don't care what you boys do in your spare time. So long as you're careful and respectful."

"It's not like that Mrs… er, Dawn."

Troy turned around. "How did you even know what we were talking about, Mitch? Were you listening to our conversation the whole time?"

Mitch came closer. "I'm sorry, Troy, but I wrote my dissertation on that moment in history. The daughter of icon Marietta C George did a total mike drop. And, my god, those designs she wore at Paris fashion week. What were they… nameless, or unnamed?"

"Unnamed. And yes, they were mine," she said proudly.

He clasped a hand over his mouth. "Shut up. You designed Unnamed?"

"I did. I was trying to make a statement. Jane was about to retire and was feeling sad that she no longer fitted the mould. Turns out, I retired shortly after too, unintentionally, of course, and… with somewhat of a buyout from that awful designer Galiel. Still, being a man with an exotic name gave him a catapult over what I had already built."

"Wow, Troy, you did not tell me that your mum was a legend. Did you ever meet Marietta?"

"Just once, and not in good circumstances, I'm afraid. And unfortunately, I read in the paper that she died a few years back."

"I know, such a sad moment. So, what happened to Jane? Wait, didn't she have—"

She quickly cut him off. "I'm just telling Troy about Jane. Let's do this chronologically, shall we?"

"Gosh, sorry Dawn, this is absolutely not my business."

"No, it's not," snapped Troy. He grabbed the wine bottle and filled both of their glasses.

"Please stop being grumpy. I'm sorry about earlier, okay?"

"You've had an argument?" Dawn asked.

"Well—" said Mitch.

"No," Troy interjected. "Do you want to join us for the story, Mitch?" He sighed.

Mitch smiled coyly. "Absolutely. But I don't want to interrupt."

"You already bloody have," hissed Troy.

"Not at all, come sit," Dawn said, feeling like this was already a breakthrough.

"Grab a wine glass," said Troy. "But this is family business, not for the media."

"I know, I get it," Mitch said, grabbing a glass as instructed.

"You're a journalist?" she asked.

Mitch turned to her. "I have a little online fashion magazine called Habitude."

She watched as he gestured widely with his hands.

"It's a bit of a what's hot? What's not? Who wears it best? Callab, if you know what I mean? It started more as a blog in my own time and has grown from there, really."

"He's being modest. It's amazing. He's now on it full time and considering hiring staff. You should check it out. But, getting back to the point; I get you had your moment in the sun, Mum," he said, "but what has this got to do with me? You said you felt it was important that I heard this story."

"I promise, it's relevant."

"So, tell me more," he said, raising his eyebrows.

"Remember how, for many years, I went to Paris fashion week, and you used to come along with me to watch?"

"Yes."

"Well, the year of 2001, you were around, what, nine years old?"

He nodded.

"And you had that scout camp and couldn't join me. So, I went alone. Do you remember? My trip got extended, so your dad had to collect you, and you stayed with him?"

He leant back and popped an olive into his mouth. "Couldn't join you? It's funny how differently people remember things. I hated that camp."

"I thought you loved it. You went for, like, four years in a row. You'd go canoeing, rock climbing, play games and do obstacle courses, remember the obstacle courses?"

"I went, to make things easier on you Mum. I don't particularly remember the activities; I remember my clothes getting thrown into the lake, me being tripped up, and smacking my nose on a rock. Actually, I think I still have the scar from that." He rubbed the side of his nose as though trying to find it with his fingers.

She held a hand over her throat, felt a heat snaking up her core. "I didn't know that. Why didn't I know?"

"Erm, because I didn't tell you. You didn't have time for me, and I wanted to please you. But the kids there, were mean to me."

"I'm so sorry you were unable to tell me that!" she leant over to place a hand on his arm.

"It's in the past. But what's the god-awful camp got to do with anything?"

# Five

Dawn sipped her champagne; she had been called to Marilyn Marshall's hotel room. Marilyn was the CEO of Marshall Media, global events planners and winners of the Warner Award for their TV show, *The Fix*, a show about real drug addicts on the street of Glasgow. If Marilyn was involved, Dawn knew this had to be a big deal. Not only that but sat beside her was a small bunch of people who looked as though they too had also been dragged from the event. *Or even bed*, she pondered, looking to her left at a model dressed in a short, black, silk pyjama set.

The room was busy with chatter, people were still arriving.

"Hi, I'm Delvin," the guy next to her in a blue shirt said. "Are you a designer?"

"Yes."

"Me too. I've been creating bridal wear for about twelve years now. I also work in a gym in my spare time."

She turned and glanced over his physique. He looked like he had a gym body. A woman in a white jacket and a hijab seemed to appear from nowhere.

"Yes, we always need a secure job on top, don't we?" She sniggered. "I've done everything from wedding make-up to working in a baker's shop in my not so spare time." She looked momentarily embarrassed. "Sorry, I'm Miryam. I'm from Los Angeles, I do mainly tailor and contour work. I'm trying to redefine sophistication."

Dawn nodded. "Redefine sophistication, eh? Nice," she replied awkwardly. They turned to look at her expectantly. Just in time, Angie, her PA, approached. She handed her a bottle of water and turned to her.

"Dawn, please don't kill me. A couple of months ago, Marilyn's assistant came into our local coffee shop. We got to talking about the show and I sort of indicated you might be interested in being part of it."

"Why?"

"It's televised. I didn't realise it would be more of a start-up thing."

Dawn turned to her. "Well, I need some inspiration for new designs, it might be interesting," she cooed.

Delvin crossed his arms; his eyes ran up and over Dawn. They darted back to Angie then back to Dawn. They stopped on her face, before widening.

"Hold on a minute," he said, pointing at her with a bent wrist. "You're Dawn Lewis." He said it accusingly.

Dawn hesitated for a moment. "I am," she replied, slowly.

She heard one of them gasp. "What are you even doing in this contest?"

"Didn't even know I was entering one. Maybe Marilyn felt I needed a boost."

"Ahh, no way. You're amazing. This must be more high

profile than we realise," replied Delvin enthusiastically.

"Yeah, if she's in this, maybe this is my big break," exclaimed Miryam."So, what's this all about, anyway? Do any of you know?" Dawn asked conspiratorially.

"Do we know?" asked Delvin, a hand pressed into his chest in mock horror. "Of course, we know. We've worked our damn asses off to get here."

"Marilyn has been talking about putting together a team of designers for a new TV show. I think they're looking for a specific design," came the voice of a woman with a half shaved, half blue hair, who was standing beside them. "I've been wanting to get my animal-free designs in front of Marilyn for a while now. I just can't seem to get her attention."

"Animal-free?"

"Yes. I want to be in the fashion business, but they're killing animals. I want to make fashion that's available for everyone, so that people can make a choice not to kill animals."

"I think that's great, but you'll really need something spectacular. Otherwise, people might see you as this sort of weird new girl."

The woman's eyes widened.

"I'm not trying to be rude. It's a tough audience out there. Don't get me wrong, if your designs are good and they're of a good quality, they could have potential. Do you have finance behind you?"

"No, that's why I need this so bad."

"Name?"

"It's... Gloria." She said her name as though it were a question.

"Not your name, the label name."

"Oh, sorry, it's Skin."

"Just Skin?"

Gloria nodded.

"Okay, so the name needs work. Do you have designs?"

"Of course."

She pulled her sketch pad out. Dawn's eyes scanned the page. Her designs weren't half bad.

"I heard this show was Sean Combs' idea." Came Delvin's chirpy voice.

Gloria turned her back to them and answered her phone. Dawn still held her notepad, wondering about this woman's chances.

"I hadn't heard anything about it until five minutes before I got here," Dawn replied to Delvin.

"Well, that's because I doubt you'd be looking for opportunities like most of us are," said Delvin, with a nod.

She watched all the young hot models and designers and wondered why Marilyn had picked her. Half of them did look fresh out of college.

Gloria hung up her call and turned back to them. Her forehead was creased in concern. "Looks like I'm out," she said, taking the notepad from Dawn. "My childminder hasn't turned up and no-one can reach my ex."

Dawn stared at her for a moment. *What if she had a chance with this animal-free stuff?*

Gloria walked away. Dawn reacted instinctively.

"Wait," she said, placing a hand on her arm. Gloria turned and looked at her.

Dawn asked, "How old is your daughter?"

"Six."

"Well, it's useless flying back to the UK now. Not only are you giving up on the chance of a lifetime, but by the time you get there, social services will have already taken her in for the night." She saw the panic in Gloria's eyes at the mention of social services.

"I can't just stay and not be there for my daughter!"

"And I'm not suggesting you do. You're from Birmingham, right? From your accent."

"Yes."

"I'm sure if we ask her nicely, Angie here will make some calls and get someone from our Coventry office to go and find your ex-husband. We have a nursery full of qualified carers for the care of our employee's kids. If we need to, we could probably get one of them to fly here with your daughter, so that she can stop here, with you."

"That sounds costly."

"It's fine. I've got you."

"You don't even know me."

"Call it a good deed."

Gloria glared at her, as though she just couldn't fathom it. Dawn exhaled.

"Look, I have the resources to help you. You might have real potential. Running out now could ruin you before you even start."

Her eyes flickered across the room and back to Dawn.

"What do you need from me?" she asked, turning to Angie.

She gave Angie as much information as she could, and Angie hurried off. Gloria stood rubbing her arms, goose bumps covering them despite the heat.

"Relax. Angie will sort it. Honestly, she's like the

modern age Albert Einstein of problem solving."

Gloria turned to her, with eyes full of tears. "I don't know what I did to deserve your help. But thank you. I will pay you back."

"Honestly, it's fine. You can pay me back when your brand is thriving."

Gloria grinned at her. "Deal." She sighed. "I often wonder if I should give it all up to be a better mother. But why do I need to choose between my dreams and being a good mum?"

"You shouldn't. That's one reason men are running the show."

"It's just so hard. How do you do it with three kids to think of?"

"Well, for a start, my ex-husband is an amazing father. Always has been. He would never go AWOL when he needs to be available."

Gloria blushed. "That must be nice."

"It's how it should be. You're both parents." She shook her head. "God, I hated Michael when we first broke up. A single mother at forty, I thought I was screwed. Turns out, I'm better without him. Now I'm kind of grateful he cheated. We were never suited. Not really."

"You never met anyone else?"

"Not yet. I don't have time for a relationship. I'm not even sure what my type would be." It didn't stop her imagination from conjuring up scenarios, though.

"I know my type." Gloria said. "I totally imagine myself with someone who looks surprisingly like Colin Egglesfield."

There was a collective giggle around the group.

Dawn had been with her husband for twenty years. She couldn't remember if he was her type when they met, but she knew for sure he wasn't by the time they split. What even was her type? The figure she'd imagined was nameless and faceless. It was just a blur. It was the actions of the figure that she'd been fantasising about. The indefinable blur jogging beside her around a lake or on a beach, sitting in a nice restaurant drinking red wine or eating a plate of fish or pasta, laughing with her, their body language pointed towards one another. Sometimes she imagined them just cuddling on the sofa, making fun out of bad TV, a fireplace blazing in the background. Either way, in the scenarios, a shadow filled the space. The one thing she knew was that they wore each other like old slippers. She'd never felt like that with Michael, she'd never felt like he was her equal, she felt boring by his side.

Marilyn coughed, pulling her from her thoughts, she looked around the room and Dawn pivoted on her heel.

"Good evening, everyone," she called over the crowd. "I know it was of short notice my requesting you be here, but what I want to discuss with you is time-sensitive. So, as a thank you, on your way out, please help yourselves to a goodie bag."

There were a few whispers around the room. Marilyn's goodie bags were customary, known for being thousands of pounds' worth of branded freebies. The press usually ate them up.

"Okay, then let's begin. I have only requested the company of those whom I know and trust, and if you look around the room, you may notice that with us this evening we have: eight quality journalists, eight fantastic designers and…" She counted with her finger. "Six models. Oh, two appear to have not yet made it. Anyhow, there is a reason for these numbers. I assume everyone signed the non-disclosure on entry?" she asked, following the nods of heads.

"So, fashion week has come to an end. But this year, we have arranged a special bonus. A Vegas show, travelling in the comfort of my private jet. We've been invited to Studio 54 by the owner to do a fashion show in the club."

There were some 'ohs' followed by a bang, and people jolted around. A young man and woman came into the room. The tall, slim, blonde woman was dressed in a smart, black tailored suit, followed by a slim young man with a square jaw and finely shaved beard, dressed in a long white shirt dress with bright green leggings.

"Wonderful, you made it out of the end of the show," Marilyn cheered. "Please, do take a seat. I was just telling these fine young people about our commencing trip to Las Vegas. So, as I was saying, each designer will need to create a piece of clubwear for their designated model. The winner gets a clothing contract for a yearly Vegas fashion show for the next consecutive five years. The good news is, you will have full access to any materials and equipment you may need. However, you do have only…" She looked at her watch. "Thirty-eight hours to complete two outfits. One casual daytime, one evening clubwear. Let me know now if you have commitments and are unable to join us. We will be in Vegas for four days."

The room became a mush of concerned and excited chatter. Marilyn raised her voice over them, and hands rose amongst the small crowd.

"I will answer questions at the end. I just want to say, the whole process and nightclub show will be televised. There are singers and celebrities attending by invite only, but we already have Sean Combs."

"Yass, I knew it," hissed Delvin beside her.

"Shakira and Alicia Keys are also on our agreed list, and I do know that Samuel Colton Jr is trying to free his schedule to join."

"So, she bagged Colton then?" the voice beside her said.

"Do you know he has classic designs created for him and wears them on every red carpet? I've tried so many times to get that man to wear my designs. He's loyal to a fault," said Miryam.

"He's at his peak in his acting career, too. Getting him now would triple your label, Dawn."

She turned to where the voice had come from. Beside her was a small pale face, a face she recognised.

"Well, I never. Tom Woodley." She grinned and rocked back on her heels. "How on earth did you get dragged into this?"

He side-eyed her. "I could ask you the same thing."

"I didn't even know I was getting entered into a bloody contest. I'm still not sure why I'm here."

He turned and looked at her then. "Oh, you really don't know." He grinned.

"What?"

"What rock have you been hiding under?" he asked with a snigger. "This is Marilyn's party trick. She mixes experienced and non-experienced designers and journalists and puts them in the ring together, so they can brawl it out." He jostled.

"But that puts the newbies at a massive disadvantage," she said imperiously.

He edged closer and spoke downwards. "She claims that it not only motivates the up-and-comers, but that it also stops the professionals from becoming complacent."

Dawn chewed at her lip.

"Of course, what it actually does," he said on an inhale, "is creates animosity. The animosity, of course, is where Marilyn really finds her spark. Thus, fodder for a televised audience and our friend Marilyn here gets a top reality show from the emotions of professionals chasing her carrot for their livelihood."

"Brutal," Dawn breathed.

"But also, kind of genius, isn't it?" He grinned.

"If evil can be classed as genius, I suppose. Have any of her subjects ever stepped up the career ladder from these so-called contests?"

"Oh, absolutely. Patsy Loo, Gina Parker and Graham Bennett are all of her making."

"Really? They're of her making?" she whispered.

"Yes. And you know what they have in common, Dawn?"

"What's that?"

"None of them got sucked into the politics and drama. You're a good person, Dawn. Stay your usual placid self and you will be fine. You may well lose the contest, but you'll certainly win the long game."

"Hmmm, makes you feel like walking away. Why do you do it, Tom? You're an established journalist."

He pinched his chin thoughtfully. "You're an established designer, Dawn. But you're still here, still considering it.

Being around all these designers and models, the fact it's being televised… it's publicity, good or bad, is it not?"

"I suppose," she said, sitting down. "And, my god, I would love to get a contract with Samuel Colton Jr. But I'm not into getting back in the ring with all these youngsters."

She heard a voice over the other side of the room calling Tom. He glanced over, then he leant in and kissed Dawn on the cheek.

"Good luck," he mouthed, walking away.

Dawn moved forwards through the crowd of chattering people. She took a seat on a small bench and looked around until her eyes blurred in thought. No longer able to hear the noises around the room, her brain begun to accumulate ideas. She pulled her pad and pencil from her bag and immediately her fingers danced over the blank canvas. This would be a nice change, and a massive boost for her brand, whether or not she enjoyed competing with newbies. Maybe she could even be of help.

# Six

Jane dialled the number for her publicist, Leoni, and tapped her manicured nail against her cheek.

"Leoni? Bella Bernstein just came to my room."

"Oh?" came back a sleepy voice.

"Apparently, I've been commanded to her majesty's quarters."

Leoni made a panicked squeak of a sound; Jane then heard a bang before Leoni replied. "I'll be outside your room in two minutes." There was a thud. Jane giggled.

Within minutes, Leoni came racing into the corridor. She was wearing a three-quarter length jacket with a wrist full of jingling bracelets, her tight, black, curly hair tied up in a small ponytail on top of her head. Her face was pale.

"You alright?" Jane asked her. "Awhh, don't tell me you went out last night after the crazy day we had?"

They both strode towards the lift.

"I'm fine." She gulped nervously. "Of course not! The only thing I was doing last night was sorting through your enquiries."

"So, what's this whole fing about anyway? Do you know anything?" she asked Leoni.

They stepped into the lift; Jane hit the button for the top floor. She turned to look at Leoni.

"What's with the face, Le?

"So..." She squirmed.

"Oh god, what?" She put a hand on her hip.

"When you were on stage, Marilyn's assistant... Perry, is it?"

Jane shrugged.

"Well, anyway, her assistant came in and asked for names for a TV contest."

The lift stopped. A woman in a black Dior dress, with long, silky, straight blonde hair, stepped on. They all nodded at each other sagely. She pressed floor fourteen. And Leoni quietened her voice.

"I offered your name up."

Jane turned to Leoni, her cat's eyes squinting, making her high cheekbones even more prominent. She pushed back on her already flat hair.

"Look, I know you're trying to get out. I just thought you could do one last public stint. It might at least give you some options, you know?" she whispered.

Jane kept her lips pursed. They both stood in silence as the lift moved up. Jane kept glancing at Leoni as though she wanted to say something. Leoni looked at her pleadingly.

The lift doors opened, and the woman stepped off.

Jane looked at Leoni and tapped her foot. "What even is this thing?"

Leoni turned to her. "It's a TV show. But it's real life. Marilyn Marshall is the creator, and it's to win a contract with Studio 54. And I know you're readying yourself for retirement, I do. But win or lose, this would get you some great publicity."

They stepped out of the lift.

"And I want publicity because…?"

Jane swayed down the corridor, taking large strides. Leoni shuffled behind her, walking double steps in an attempt to keep up.

"Because, I was thinking that if your name remains in the public eye, then maybe you could do a few TV ads in the future, a few guest appearances here and there… you know, just small parts to keep a bit of cash flow going."

Jane stopped sharply, turned around, and looked at her. "Come on, Le," she whined. "You know that ain't what I want."

Leoni put her hand up defensively and together they walked again.

"Look, I know. I know, you don't want to be your mum and I'm not trying to continue your career like that. But Jane, once your name disappears from the public eye, the income is over too. And the likelihood is, it won't come back. This way we get to keep you in their memories just enough to take you to a more realistic retirement age, but not so much that you can't gain the independence you're after."

"To be honest, Leoni, I'm past caring."

"You might think that now. But when it's gone, there's no getting it back."

"God, is that what it comes to? A woman gets to forty, and she's forced into tacky TV to survive."

"When that woman is a supermodel, then sometimes, yes."

"Well, aren't I just a drop in the ocean?" She guffawed, pushing through the swinging doors and letting them fall behind.

She marched forwards. Leoni chased after her.

"It's this door," she said, directing Jane to the left.

Jane stopped, her face close to the doors. She lifted her entire body in a swan-like motion, tugged at the bottom of her jacket and opened the double doors with a quiet air of grace as she entered the busy room.

Leoni scanned the room. She pointed out who was who, then pulled a sheet of paper from her laptop bag. Reading from it, she said, "So, they teamed you with journalist Terry Mack and designer…." She flipped the page. "Dawn Lewis."

She looked at Leoni. "D-Lay?" She raised her eyebrows. "I could do worse, I s'pose."

"Yeah, I looked her up. She's not a bad designer either. She's dressed some pretty famous people over the years, and she's also experienced like you, so you should gel well."

"By experienced, you mean old." She laughed. "I hear she's got a stick up her arse as well. Will we 'gel' from that, too?"

"You shouldn't believe everything you hear."

"Wise." She snorted. "Then let's go and find her."

They walked slowly through the crowds, glancing around.

"I think I can see her over there, on the back row."

Jane followed Leoni; she watched her stride confidently through the crowd. People glanced over Leoni dismissively, some eyes landing on Jane with smiles of recognition.

Leoni stopped by a chair at the back, a woman was hunched over her notepad and hadn't even noticed them standing so close to her. She was wearing tight jeans with ballet pumps, a silky pink top and a grey suit jacket with a scarf around her neck, looking almost as thin as the models she worked with. Her hair was balled up on top of her head and was wobbling around as she scribbled ferociously. "Dawn Lewis?" asked Leoni.

The woman peered up and blew away a strand of fallen hair from her face. Their eyes locked and Jane felt her stomach tighten. There was something beautifully poetic about the busy hall and this woman's natural beauty, as she violently scribbled out the images from her mind.

***

Dawn heard her name. She looked up, not expecting plastic Jane to be standing there staring at her. Their eyes locked, and she suddenly felt something. What was that? Irritation? A tummy bug? Nerves?

Jane George was renowned in the modelling world for having no personality. She was stiff and un-human-like, according to the media. Yet standing in front of her, the woman told a different story. A glowing complexion of peach skin, high cheekbones and a thin slash of green eyes that sparkled with mischief. Something strangely irritated Dawn about this intrusion. She tugged off her suffocating scarf. When had she gotten so hot and frustrated?

"Dawn, I'm Leoni Robinson, this is Jane George. I believe we're being teamed up." The fake enthusiasm in Leoni's voice wasn't lost on Jane.

"Apparently so," Dawn said, rising from her seat.

She shook their hands, feeling unusually rigid with Jane's eyes burning into her.

Dawn met Jane's gaze. "We haven't met before, have we? I assume you're just so familiar to me, from the media and the shows I've worked on."

"I'd have thought so. Although I do love your handbags, Dawn Lewis."

"They're our bestsellers. I'll get you one," she said, with a wink.

"Excellent, thanks."

"I think your mum had a few when she was on the catwalk herself. How is she these days? She doesn't seem around as much anymore."

"Oh, she's still around alright," she said, with a raise of the brows. Everyone loved to hear all about her mother, they saw her modelling, dishing out free fashion advice. She was everywhere at one stage, cooking shows, exercise DVDs, you name it. She'd even written a book. Jane loved her mother to death but talking about her had become boring. People always wanted to know the same things.

"Actually, did I notice a novel being advertised recently?" she asked, rising from her seat.

Jane internally rolled her eyes, trying to look interested. "You probably did." She smiled. "It's a bare all book about the industry, enlightening the world to the beauty and evil of modelling.""I don't think she will ever quit. What an absolute legend. Mind you, I bet you didn't think that growing up, hey?"

She smiled at that. "I can't even complain that she was

an absent mother. She was Marietta C George to everyone else, but mum to me – always there when I needed her."

"Beautiful! I hope my kids say that about me one day."

"I'm sure they will."

"So, tell me about your preferred style, Jane."

She pulled her eyes away, switching to business mode. This was just another day at the office. Another client needing a design, she told herself. She explained how she worked and made notes when Jane spoke. She always automatically swept her eyes along a client's body, evaluating their shape and size in her mind, she'd usually been able to guess what kind of style would look good on them based on their shape and size, but suddenly she felt unable to. Suddenly, she felt embarrassed about running her eyes down Jane's body. Worried that she was hovering. What was going on with her?

Jane's hair looked thick and healthy, and her body was lean, rather than under-nourished. There was a softness to her face that Dawn hadn't expected. Like there was something deeper, something further highlighted by her casual t-shirt and jeans. Dawn reached her eyes; Jane was looking at her, too. Curiosity in her eyes, as though she too was evaluating Dawn.

"Well, aren't I honoured?" a loud voice came. "I didn't even know how I'd sneak onto this thing, and here I am being given an exclusive."

They both turned as the man swept in with hugs and kisses all around. Jane looked taken aback.

"Terry Mack, *The Look*."

Dawn welcomed him into a hug. "Pleased to meet you, Terry."

Leoni shook his hand. "I'm Leoni, Jane's publicist. Nice to meet you."

"You too. Wow, they don't just give me one beautiful woman, but three. Honestly, what did I do to deserve this?"

"I'm wondering the same thing."

They all turned to look at Jane as she spoke.

"You look like you only just came out of uni." Jane felt bad whilst the words were still falling from her lips, and yet she continued. Why was she being rude to this stranger? She didn't know why, but she'd taken an instant disliking to him.

Terry turned to her and rubbed his face. "Just good genes, I'm afraid." He didn't seem offended in the slightest.

"And from what I've seen, you're breaking barriers in the media." Dawn spoke up. "Jane, honestly, if you'd seen Terry's work. He has such honest portrayals and flawless attention to detail, it's refreshing."

Terry put an arm over her shoulder and side-eyed her. "Well, thank you, Dawn. I'm impressed with your work, too."

Jane rolled her eyes, like a petulant teen, and Dawn smiled. Terry Mack was a tall man, with the physique of a rugby player. He wore a collared blue Ralph Lauren top with grey joggers and had floppy hair and a boyish cheeky charm about him, and she could see herself being charmed by him.

He leant towards Jane. "I actually assisted Marietta C George a couple of years ago when she was advertising her callisthenics DVD," he said.

She glared back at him unimpressed.

"And Dawn…" he continued, turning to face her. "You're like an angel. You stayed so classy through that whole cheating husband thing. I'd have sold that bastard's story to the press within hours."

She laughed. "Well, that's nice of you, Terry, but he is the father of my children."

"Like I say, classy, as well as beautiful."

"Designers, models and journalists." Marilyn called over the room. "Let's do this." She stomped out of the room, everyone following her.

"I was hoping to get home for my birthday tomorrow as well." Jane sighed.

"Ahh, did James have a big celebration planned for you?"

Dawn watched her gulp and play with her fingers nervously.

"Yeah, I'm sure I'll be missing out on a big celebration with all of my friends and family."

"We'll have some cocktails after the show," suggested Leoni.

"Yeah," agreed Dawn.

They marched in line along the corridor and up the stairs. Terry walked beside Dawn and Leoni. Jane was in front.

"Have you worked as Jane's publicist for long, Leoni?"

Leoni turned to him. "Just a couple of years. I run a company called Medbourne Creations. We run the PR for several people in the fashion industry."

"Is she hard work?"

"Actually, she's a delight to work for," she said, sounding genuine. "One of my easiest clients."

He eyed her suspiciously. "Don't tell me, she's a man hater."

"Not at all, Terry. Give her time. She will come around to you."

He looked at her sceptically before then turning to Dawn. "Have you been in these competitions before?"

"Not televised, and not since I was a budding intern fighting for my place in the fashion world. I didn't realise I'd be in my forties with a renowned company and still competing for my place."

They reached a door and began gliding in one by one.

"Oh, I don't think you need to compete for anything. I think she just wanted to make it a little fun. Create a media buzz. I, for one, am so excited to watch you and Jane in action."

Jane turned and looked at him then. "Well, of course you are, Terry. You actually are competing for your place in the industry."

Terry raised his eyebrows. "I've been in the industry for almost six years. I'm one of our top reporters," he said, and stepped back to follow them through a narrow archway. Jane gave him a patronising, tilted smile, which he seemed to shrug off with a wide smile in return.

The room they entered comprised eight tables and several enormous windows that looked out over the Eiffel Tower. To the end of the room was a wall of mirrored cabinets that ran the length of the space.

A man came around to them, smiling. "Can I get any of you a coffee, tea, water?"

"Coffee would be great, thanks."

"Oh, me too. I feel we may need it." Terry laughed. He

opened his notebook and got comfy in the chair. Jane and Leoni went off in search of the toilet.

Dawn sat at the table with a tiny pencil gripped in her hand, and she moved it dramatically over the paper.

"So, Dawn, do you have any, like, rituals or inspirations that get your juices flowing, so to speak?" asked Terry.

She spoke, her eyes remaining on the page. "Erm, well, I do insist on my room smelling of Coco Chanel." She paused. "I like a fresh bunch of tulips for each room. And, of course, there's the pot of Kopi Luwak I like to have readily prepared."

"Really? Kopi Luwak, is that flown in especially?" he asked, whilst absently scribbling down notes at lightning speed. She stopped her sketching and stared at the top of his head with a grin. "No. Not really. None of that is true. Who drinks that shit anyway?"

He paused his pen, discretely scribbling out what he had written, and he stared at her- their eyes fixing.

"Literal cat shit," he barked out with a burst of laughter.

She grinned. "Can't believe you were so easily willing to accept that, whilst acting as though it was a totally normal thing to say."

"Hey, if you'd seen the things I've seen, you'd take nothing for granted."

They grinned at each other, and in that moment, she felt a likeness to him. Her eyes studied his face. *He looks kind*, she thought, *for a journalist*. Like someone she could laugh with, and she wouldn't feel judged or berated.

She looked away and stretched both of her arms into the air, wiggling her fingers.

"No, I can honestly say that a mind that isn't too busy is all I need. Sometimes I'll play a bit of Bebel Gilberto or jazz on my headphones, nothing specific, just whatever I'm listening to that day."

He looked at her thoughtfully then, his smile warm, his grey eyes seeming to take in every bit of her. She thought he must be good at pulling information from people, making them feel important enough to want to share.

"Keeping it simple," he said with a nod. "I like that."

"Hi, I'm Charlie. Pleased to meet you." A man with a camera held up on his shoulder stopped by and shook their hands. He smiled at them all before lifting the camera back up and taking a step back.

"So, Dawn, you were explaining to me how you wash your clothes?" Terry said, nodding at her encouragingly.

She looked at him, and he winked conspiratorially.

He was playing a game, she was impressed.

"Yes, I wash the synthetic blends in warm water on a gentle cycle with a gentle detergent," she replied with a grin.

"Any detergent in particular?" he asked quickly.

She stuttered; she was dying to laugh. The moment their eyes connected; she covered her laugh with a cough. She looked up, just in time to see Charlie walking away, his camera poised on someone else, and together they quietly giggled.

"You're so bad."

"Got to play them at their own game." He winked. "Right, let's get back to it. So, you're ready to launch for autumn/winter soon, aren't you?" he asked, with a sparkle in his eye.

She leant forwards, amused by this man. "I am, and I'm really excited about it, too. We've got glitter and lace and some very sexy silk coming… just watch this space."

"Oh, I will," he purred. "I'm very excited to see how you dress Jane over the next forty-eight hours too. You've dressed Kate Winslet in the past, haven't you?" He raised his eyebrows as though impressed.

"Are you kidding? Jane is a beauty, she's no contest at all. But yes, I dressed Kate, along with others." She leant back and smiled at him. "It was only last spring that I dressed Cate Blanchett for a massive charity event. I also dressed Zoe Ball for several months when she was on *The Big Breakfast*. If you're old enough to remember that, that is."

"Of course, I am," he said, pushing the hair to the side that had fallen over his face.

"And more recently, Rachel Weisz, for her premier."

He sat back and folded his legs, matching her stance with a grin, fascinated by the proud gleam in her eye.

# Seven

Jane rubbed her hands dry on the fluffy, white hand towel. She felt the buzz of her phone in her pocket. Slipping it out, she exited the bathroom. It was James.

James: *Why didn't you tell me, Gizmo?*

Jane: *Tell you what?*

James: *The big 4-0! Tomorrow!!*

Jane: *You're my husband. You need reminding??*

James: *Jane, I've been as busy as hell, creating the life we dreamed of. A little heads up doesn't hurt whilst I'm working eighty-hour weeks.*

Jane: *'Dreamed' being the operative word.*

Jane meandered out of the toilet, staring at the screen. Nothing came back.

She could hear Terry and Dawn talking. She wondered if they were flirting. It was certainly heading that way. She contemplated that; being a third wheel was all she needed right now. She stopped beside them, chewing her thumbnail. She leant against the wall with her eyes glued to her phone. She felt the need to stretch or run or something.

"Ready to see my ideas now?" Dawn asked excitedly.

Jane slid the phone back into her pocket. "You have ideas? Already? Bloody hell fire."

"Well, they still need a lot of work. But yeah, I've sketched up a few ideas."

Jane's eyes glistened as she sat down with a swing of her hair. "Hit me with it, baby."

Terry leant back in his chair, watching them with interest.

Jane leant close to Dawn, looking through her tiny sketches of different outfits.

"You really are talented," she breathed. "I adore this dress. But…" She paused. "It just isn't me." She passed the notepad back.

"In what sense?" Dawn asked, squinting.

"Can't you just trust me and redesign something more suited to my figure?"

"It's only a draft. What do you mean by more suited to your figure? It's literally designed to show off your assets. Look here and here." She pointed at the page. "And if you'd prefer, we can pull this in a bit around the legs?"

"You obviously don't understand."

"Excuse my bluntness, but I think your whole body is an asset," blurted Terry. "How do you stay so toned?"

She rolled her eyes, what was it about this man that annoyed her so much? She put two fingers in her mouth and mock heaved.

"Please don't talk like such a kiss-arse." She sighed.

***

Dawn smirked, side-eyeing Terry. She was pleased to see he looked more amused than insulted. Jane sat at the table and ran a finger around the knots of the wood, then glanced at him, beneath her lashes.

"If you must know, I used to be into gymnastics, in a big way. I thought I'd make the finals for a while there, but… well, anyway, as a model, I've spent time hiding the muscular lines of my body and showing only the more delicate feminine parts. And this dress…" She turned to look at Dawn a little sadly. "Well, it won't do that."

"Damn right it won't," said Dawn.

"Then it won't work for me."

"Believe it or not, I think it's time to flaunt those beautiful lines."

"It's a fact, Dawn. I am older and broader than any of the other women in here. Standing out further would be a mistake, you should know that, given your apparent expertise."

Dawn had been insulted before, but she'd never had her experience questioned in such a way. She felt a fog developing in her head.

"Apparent?" she asked. "Why would it be a mistake? You think because you're a little older, a little stronger, that you should shrink into the background? No way, you're lean and beautiful."

"You think you know what's best for me? You think you know what it's time for, for me?"

"I think you need to trust me and do your damn job. Look, I don't know if you follow my designs, but my latest campaign is all about appreciating individuality." *Why was this woman fighting her on this?*

"I'm aware of that, but that's not going to do me any favours now, is it?" She stopped talking and looked behind Dawn angrily. "Look, maybe this was a mistake," she said through clenched teeth. Dawn turned to see Charlie with the camera pointed at them. She quickly smiled and looked back at Jane.

"Maybe we should head somewhere more private so that you can look at my ideas," she said, forcing a smile.

"Nope, that's okay, thanks," she replied, getting up from the bench.

"Where are you going?"

"I need a minute." She walked away.

Dawn turned to Terry and screwed up her face.

"Talk about proving the diva theory," he mumbled behind his hand. His voice seemed to loosen the thick air and Dawn laughed along, but she couldn't get rid of the heaviness in the pit of her stomach.

"She didn't seem like a diva when I met her." She blew out a long exhale, then looked at him. "If I knew I was going to have to deal with temper tantrums, I might as well have stayed home with the kids."

He said, "in fairness to her, she doesn't have a reputation for being a pain. If anything, she has no reputation at all. People around the media even go so far as to say she has no personality. I think we saw something very rare tonight."

She looked at him curiously. "Oh, I've heard they name her plastic Jane. Maybe there's more to her than they think."

"There usually is." He sighed.

"But she's not very kind to you." She said with a smirk.

"She's a softy compared to some people I work with. Honestly, I have skin thicker than the front of those chunky heels some of them wear around here."

She took the coffee handed to her and wrapped her hands around it, with a smile. She was staring to relax around this man.

***

Jane pulled the hood of her parka over her head to hide her face. It was a dank evening, and the streets were busy with people hurrying from day jobs and university. She wandered the cobbled streets dazed, taking in slow, soothing breaths. Was this where her life fell apart? Her career and her relationship were both coming to an end, and she'd finally lost control of her emotions in front of a damn journalist, of all people. Had any of the other journalists, models, or designers seen her lose her cool? She had no idea who she was or which direction to go in. The media and public would drop and forget her as quickly as they'd swept her up, and yet, she'd revolved her whole life around being exactly what they'd always wanted her to be.

Her mother's words echoed in her mind, *'you can only live in my shadows for so long, Janey. One day, you're going to have to make it on your own. If you're not careful, you'll find yourself with nothing and no-one.'* She thought she had been careful.

How would she make it on her own now? She had no idea how to be anyone but Marietta's daughter, Jane the model – 'doll-faced plastic Jane', the English rose with no visible personality. She knew what they said about her. She had, after all, orchestrated the whole thing. She didn't want to be known as a diva, a train wreck or a party animal like lots of the others got named the moment they lost a bit of self-control. She didn't even know if she'd want to stand out as an individual. She'd always kept her private life private, had always behaved meticulously in public. No-one knew the real her, and that's just the way she wanted it.

Her looks were open to ridicule and opinions by the world, she knew that. She was in control of her body and what she put in it, or on it, but she couldn't bear the thought of people judging the person she was. She was terrified of what they might discover about her, especially those thoughts and feelings that she couldn't afford to admit, even to herself. She was sick to death of being everyone else's bloody puppet. Dawn Lewis could go to hell, she decided. Who did she think she was, telling her what she should wear? Marietta C George would have never let a designer dictate to her. Jane wasn't about to sit back and be a mug for some hotshot designer. With a fresh wind in her step, she stomped back to the hotel.

***

The hostility of the model in front of her took Dawn aback. No personality, her arse. Obviously, someone had highly misjudged this jumped up, arrogant, self-centred woman. She took a deep breath.

"Jane," she said calmly, glancing around the room to ensure Charlie the cameraman was elsewhere. "I'm not the enemy here," she murmured. "Tell you what, you give my designs a try, see how they feel on your skin and if they aren't right, then, that's fine. At least you can say that you tried."

She had thought this was going to be easy, acting cool. She didn't know the woman would be so high maintenance. The room was busy. People had glanced over, but they all seemed to be dealing with their own dramas.

"Look at you, acting all innocent, Dawn Lewis." She laughed. "I'm at the end of my career here and you want to use me as a stepping stone into a new market? Ha. No, thanks."

"No offense, Jane, but I don't need you as a stepping stone."

Jane folded her arms and leaned back, she stared at Dawn and pursed her lips.

"My career took off long ago. If anything, I'd be using you as an example of beauty out of the box."

"Beauty out of the box. Now that is a marvellous idea. Isn't it, Jane?" whispered Terry.

Jane glared at him, then turned back to Dawn.

"No offense to you, Dawn, but you'd think you would know the fashion world by now. There's no room for differences. Differences are the reason I was never an influence, like my mother. In fact, if I'm honest, I'm surprised I've even lasted this long. S'pose I'll never know if it was all because of her fame. But that doesn't make me a pushover for people like you."

Dawn looked around the room consciously, then leant in and murmured, "I don't see you as a pushover. And so what if your career was because of your mum? Most celebrities are there by chance."

"Pah, easy for you to say, darlin'," she replied.

Dawn was eyeing Charlie as he moved closer.

"You don't have everybody judging every tiny thing you do, and I'll have you know I work damned hard for what I have." Jane's voice was raising. She was clearly oblivious.

"I don't doubt it. And I may not have everyone judging me as a person," Dawn whispered with a smile, "but I do have them judging my work, telling me how they would do it better. And you know what, Jane? These people are essentially our customers. Without them, there would be no you or me."

"I don't want their opinions. I'm a bloody human."

"Then maybe modelling isn't for you."

"Maybe it's not. How would I know?"

"That's for you to figure out. In the meantime, take what will make you grow, let the rest go. Don't listen to those saying women should be small. They want us in the background. And hell, if you're retiring anyway, why not go out with a bang?"

Leoni got to her feet, and when Dawn saw that she was blocking the hovering camera, she smiled to herself. She was really beginning to like the girl. Jane stared at her for a long moment, contemplating her words, their eyes locked. She could see the rise and fall of Dawn's chest and realised that her own breaths were heavy too. Designers usually did their jobs and minded their business. However, she knew that the annoying woman had a point. Why did women need to make themselves petite to be feminine? Why did men have to be big to be masculine? She could be a part of the message, too; she could show as much of herself as she liked. This was, after all, like she said, her last public show. A fission of excitement ran over her core and through her ribs, and she felt her lips curve into a smile. Maybe this was the purpose she'd been looking for.

"Okay," she said with a raise of her eyebrows. "Fine, I'm in."

# Eight

Terry sat with Dawn in the studio whilst she worked on her designs. Jane had gone to bed hours ago. As she worked, Terry took a few photos, asked a few questions, but when she was in the zone, he automatically sensed his time to be silent, watching the expressions on her face as she put together another masterpiece.

It was after 4am, and the room was almost empty. Terry was sat on the wooden bench to the side, writing ferociously into a notepad.

"Terry?" she croaked into the darkened room.

"Yeah?" he replied, looking up and rubbing the back of his neck.

"Why are you still up?"

She saw his smile. "Watching the creative process. And might I say, it's fascinating."

"I'm relentless and obsessed. I know. It must be boring as hell."

"Not at all."

"Well, anyway, I'm pretty much at a standstill until Jane gets out of bed. I need her measurements." She stretched out her arms with a yawn.

"Then maybe it's time you tried to get a little sleep yourself."

She glanced at the dress. "Actually, I wonder..." She reached for a piece of silk. She laid it on the table. She opened a marker pen and clamped it between her teeth whilst she stretched the material out.

From the corner of her eye, she caught Terry's head nodding, then springing back up. He was falling asleep. She looked over and smiled before going back to work. Soon she heard a squeak of the door. Jane walked in and scanned the room; she was stepping up on chairs and looking in the corners of the room.

"Everything okay, Jane?" she asked, peering after her.

"Is Charlie around?" Jane whispered.

"He left. I think he got bored around 3am watching Delvin look for his marker pen. I swear that kid spends more time looking for his lost property than he does working."

Terry got up and flicked the kettle on, then he twisted around.

"Hey, happy birthday, Jane!" he said, taking three mugs from the cupboard, spooning out instant coffee.

"Shhh, forget that. Listen, I need to talk to you both. Have you seen the show they're making about us?"

"What show?"

"The show."

"But we haven't officially started yet, have we?"

"We're being aired already."

"What? Nooo."

"Honestly, my sister reckons they're making us sound like a bunch of morons."

"How? Why?"

"Recording, editing and cutting clips of our conversations."

"No, that can't be right."

"Can't it? You wanna hear what my sister told me?"

"What about?"

"She reckons you and me were arguing. That you were shouting at me, 'your mother made you what you are.' I was screaming back, 'I don't need you and your designs.' Another one of you saying, 'you're not like the other models. You have to be tiny to be feminine.'"

Dawn's eyes widened. "What? That's not what I said."

"Well, they were the words we used, but they've took 'em completely out of context, ain't they?!"

"And made me sound like a monster."

"I think they made Delvin look all wrong as well, cus apparently he's on there, sneaking around at night looking through other people's drawings and muttering something about winning."

"He loses everything!" she exclaimed, her eyes boring into Jane.

"I know that. That Miryam woman is on there 'n' all, apparently arguing with the blue-haired woman."

"Gloria? I've not even heard them argue. They seem to get on great."

"I know."

"They aren't allowed to do that. It's defamatory."

"Oh, but they are darlin', I checked that little non-disclaimer they had us sign. Apparently, anything they air can be cut and edited for…" She put her fingers up and air quoted. "'Entertainment reasons, as they do so wish.' Mate, we haven't got a leg to stand on. Dawn, this is everything I have fought not to become. They're ruining my reputation."

"Mine too! This is exactly what he said they'd do."

"Who?" they both asked.

"Tom Woodley." She sighed his name. "He told me that Marilyn tries to create drama. He told me not to be dragged into it or it would ruin my career."

"Great. Thanks for warning us, now it's too blooming late, ain't it?"

"But hang on… we have a journo on our side."

Terry looked over, jingled the spoon into the mug without a word.

"What good's he gonna do?" she said, with a roll of the eyes.

"Surely you can do something, Terry? Can't you?"

He lifted the boiling kettle and poured water into the mugs. "I'd love to help, Dawn. I really would. But I can't see how."

"No, me neither. If only we could somehow expose the genuine conversations too."

"I have a camera. But there's no channel for that. The best thing you can do is act your arses off from now on."

"Then that's what we will need to do."

"And I will keep a full record of all of your conversations in that room from now on, maybe get some others in there too. You never know, maybe one day we will get the chance to expose them ourselves."

Dawn said, "Anything's worth a try, Terry."

He handed them a coffee each, then went over to wipe the surface down before picking up his own. Jane turned to Dawn and looked into her eyes.

"Dawn, it got me thinking about how rude I was to you though."

Dawn turned to her, surprised by the admission.

"I think we got off on the wrong foot. I'm sorry for my behaviour, I…"

Dawn's face softened. "It's okay. I think maybe we both did," she murmured, hugging her coffee mug close to her chest.

Jane put a hand on Dawn's arm, sending her nerve endings into overdrive. "I'm happy to try your designs. I'm happy to work together amicably. Can we try this again? Please?"

"At this point, I think it's the only option we have," she said, facing her. Her eyes studied Jane's face.

Terry yawned. "Well, if I'm not interrupting anything, I think I'll go and take a little catnap."

"Of course. You must be exhausted," she stuttered.

"I am a bit; I'll catch up with you both later."

She watched as he swayed out of the door like a man after whiskey. Jane looked at her, their faces close.

"Hey, I didn't interrupt anything, did I?" she asked, giving Dawn a nudge and a wink.

"With Terry?" Dawn asked, surprised. "God no… don't talk daft." She peered over at the closing empty door.

"Well, he certainly seems interested in you."

She looked back at Jane. "Ha. I think you're imagining things. He's just a wee lad. I'd eat him alive."

"I know a crush when I see one." Jane grinned. Within seconds, she'd caught a sight in her peripheral vision and her throat hitched. "Hang on a minute. Is that what I think it is?" she gushed.

Dawn nodded proudly. "It's the dress."

"Oh, my. It's beautiful, Dawn. I didn't know you'd finished it."

"Oh, it's nowhere near complete. There are pins all around it holding it into place. I just couldn't adjust the sizes. This mannequin is way out, so I was waiting to measure you. But… I'm so glad you like it."

Jane stood and pulled her leg over the box, placing her coffee on the floor. She turned to Dawn. "Like it? Gal, I love it." She began pulling off her pyjamas. "Let's get me measured then."

Dawn's throat dried up as the clothes dropped in front of her.

"Oh, come on, you ain't bashful, are ya?" Jane laughed.

Dawn coughed. "Of course I'm not bashful," she joked, her face getting hotter by the second. Dawn busied herself getting the clothes ready, trying to forget the image of Jane in her underwear that had imprinted on her brain.

***

Jane stood perfectly still. She looked around at the piled pieces of paper, the cut-up materials and sewing machine. She spotted the woman Dawn had helped out on their first meet and greet; she was pleased to see her with her head down, working hard. Maybe Dawn had judged her correctly, or maybe her kindness had been her inspiration, who knew?

She glanced down at Dawn, so kind and calm and currently tugging at the waistband of a bright green tight fitted shimmery skirt. Then she glanced over at the mirror. She had to admit, she looked stunning. Had she made a mistake being so quick to dismiss Dawn? She tried to imagine the reaction of the people who would be watching the show. The celebrities would probably be in their element. But then she thought about the media, the way they'd make her look. And what the newspapers were probably saying about her already, from the show. Her stomach tightened. Dawn was intriguing, not like the other designers she'd met. She was down to earth, her face was a picture of pure concentration. She had a pen hanging from her mouth and her hair was fluffed up at the fringe. But could she trust this woman not to make a fool out of her? If Dawn Lewis was this confident in her own abilities, then why had she blushed at the site of a model removing her clothes? Why had she looked so staggered when they first met? Jane herself felt in awe of Dawn. Yet Dawn acted like it was the other way around.

Dawn stopped and stepped back to look at the skirt proudly. She grabbed her coffee and took a swig, still deep in thought.

"Ooh, would you mind passing mine?" asked Jane with a stretched out arm. Dawn looked startled, as if she had forgotten Jane was even there.

"No," she said, simply.

"Huh? No, you don't mind or...?"

Dawn bent down and unpicked a bottom piece of stitch in the skirt. She grabbed a piece of yellow material from the table and brought it over.

"I mean, no. I can't risk having you get coffee on the clothes. Sorry, you will have to wait."

She stood silent for a moment. Who was this woman to tell her no?

"But it will go cold," she whispered, as Dawn gently tucked the silk fabric around her chest. Jane could read the look on Dawn's face, and she knew she wasn't getting the coffee. She was absorbed and determined.

"It is what it is," said Dawn, pulling it tight around her.

Jane looked intentionally perplexed, and Dawn held back a laugh. Jane grinned. Eventually they were both struggling to contain a case of childlike giggles.

Dawn walked away, wiped the tears of laughter from her face and scrambled through a box of accessories.

"What are you looking for?" asked Jane.

"I don't think the bustier is tight enough to really make the skirt have a massive impact. Maybe I should have used a tighter material than silk." She looked thoughtful for a moment. "I think I'm going to try a string, cut out a piece in the back and use it to pull the bustier in, to tighten it."

"It already looks effective to me."

"We're going bigger here, Jane," she said, pulling a piece of string from the box. "You know, I always wanted to do a dress like this in the past. I just never thought the world was ready for the peacock look."

She went over, pulling at the bustier; Jane felt her rib cage as it was yanked to submission.

"And I'm glad I waited, because now is just the perfect time to make our statement. And you are the perfect model for it. Right, take it off. I need to stitch the string in."

Jane removed it. "It's really pretty." She exhaled.

"Well, pretty won't cut it. We're going for spectacular," she marvelled, picking up the scissors and hacking into the bustier. Jane strolled around the room, pulling a plain t-shirt on over her head. She peered out of the window into the darkness as she stretched out her arms.

"Here, come help. You can choose where you want the opening."

She turned and obeyed, wanting to be involved in the process.

They stitched in the string together, adding material, creating a bigger gap. It was still dark outside when Delvin walked in.

"Heyyy, ladies. Looking good," he said, eyeing the dress with a smile.

"Hi, Delvin." They both smiled back at him.

Miryam came in next and got straight to work. Neither of them had noticed the sun beginning to rise outside.

Before long, Terry entered the room, humming to himself. He was dressed in khaki trousers with a utility shirt; he was looking a little fresher. His hair was, however, standing on end, and he was biting into some kind of weird, packaged meat. Dawn was crouched over the sewing machine; Jane was sitting back, sewing. She glanced up at the clock. It was 7am, there was light streaming in through the window.

"Wow, I can't believe we've been working on this all night," she said, waking from a fog. Dawn looked up from the machine. Her eyes were red, her hair was standing on end. Jane thought how sweet she looked, all sleepy and confused. Her eyes ran over her face and stopped on her full lips. For a moment she wondered how it would feel to kiss Dawn, how it would feel to nibble her bottom lip and how her skin would feel against her own.

She blinked and widened her sleepy eyes. A sudden realisation of her thoughts, she wanted to lift her shoulders to relieve the feeling of pressure building in her chest. But she realised that Terry was watching her. He was watching her, watching Dawn, a look of scrutiny in his eyes. She felt self-conscious.

Terry turned away. He glanced around the studio, his eyes wandering amongst the fabric slung over the chairs and mannequins and even the sewing machine and at the enormous pile of long black feathers.

"So, I see," he said with a smile.

She noticed his eyes widen in surprise at the designs that Dawn had almost completed.

"How did you come up with these details in such a short space of time?" he asked.

She wondered if he'd read her mind. If he was covering it up. Or if he genuinely admired Dawn the way he seemed to.

"It's what I do," Dawn said simply.

Jane watched as they smiled at each other. Was there something there between them?

"Plus, I've had help. I don't know what I would have done without Jane if I'm honest," she said, clamping a bunch of feather stalks between her teeth.

He looked at Jane and smiled. "Well, you've both done amazingly. Why don't you get an hour of shut-eye, and come back to it when you're feeling fresh?"

Dawn spoke to him through gritted teeth. "See, if you knew me, Terry." Pause. "You would know that." Pause. "I don't. And evidently can't… settle… until I complete the task at hand."

"If it helps, I can stitch," he offered.

She stopped what she was doing then and looked at him, removing the feather from her mouth.

"You? You can stitch?"

"I can. My mum was a leader of the local Girl Guides. I used to go along and help out."

Dawn laughed. "Well, as reassuring as your Girl Guide experience is, I've got to say I'd rather not risk it."

"I'll have you know I was a talented seamstress. And I promise I will do my best to serve my queen and community," he said with a grin.

Dawn clamped her hand over her mouth, her eyes widened. "You seriously memorised the Girl Guide motto?" she whispered.

"I didn't memorise it, I heard it constantly," he whined.

"You are such a geek." She grinned. "And don't think I don't trust you, but I'm funny about who touches my designs. They are my pride and joy. Especially when we only have fifteen hours until the show."

Terry coughed the words, "Control freak," and she widened her eyes at him again with a grin.

Jane smiled and stretched out her arms. "Well, I for one am bloody knackered, mate. But we're getting there ain't we, Dawny?"

Dawn nodded as Jane's eyes softly swept over her.

Terry stood up. "Maybe I can make myself useful another way. Would either of you like coffee?"

"Would I, heck. We left my last one to go stone cold," she said, eyeing Dawn. Dawn looked back at her, needle poised in front of her, and she smirked. Terry gave them an incredulous look, then walked out of the room with a shake of the head.

"Are you ready to try this one on now? I think we're almost there."

She finished the last stitch, then popped the needle into a pin cushion that was balanced precariously on the edge of the table amongst everything else. Then she held out the dress for Jane to see.

"Dawn," she gasped. "I love how you've transformed that back section. It's flipping gorgeous. Do you think it will look good on me?"

"No," she replied, absently smoothing it down with flat palms. Jane stripped off again and she peered over at her, puzzled. Their eyes met and Dawn paused. "I don't think it will look good on you, I think it will look stunning on you. You'll be the most beautiful woman in the room."

Jane gulped, her stomach whirling with nerves as their eyes locked.

Dawn's eyes widened; she quickly looked away. "And you should be, too. You're gorgeous and I'm talented," she said, leaning back in her chair and rubbing her eyes.

Jane laughed. "Well, there are lots of other gorgeous, talented people here too, funnily enough," she said, climbing into the dress. They both stood silently for a moment, marvelling at how the dress hugged her body.

Jane looked around. Charlie was pointing his camera at Miryam, who was ripping up a design with tears streaming down her face.

Dawn turned back to Jane. "Okay, take it off," she said quickly. "I don't want it spoilt. Can you try the playsuit on too?"

Jane nodded, and Dawn helped her out of the dress. Then she went over to Miryam.

***

"Everything okay?"

Miryam looked at her. "It's no good," she balled.

Dawn glanced over the A-line brown, flowered dress.

"It's got potential," Dawn murmured. "But crinoline makes it a little stiff and works better in layers. How about putting a couple of layers over the top, like this?" she said, layering a piece of material over and pinning it on. "Then adding a part here on the opposite side, so that it opens in with a fold in the middle when she walks. And if you wanted, you could put a dash of colour inside that's only seen when the model strides along the catwalk. Maybe something bright, or even shimmery for the club lights."

Miryam's tears had stained her cheeks as she watched in awe. Charlie was now over the other side of the room watching another woman complaining that her model was missing.

"I hadn't thought of that," Miryam gasped. "You're the best."

"No problem."

She made her way back over to where Jane was standing in front of the mirror in the playsuit, watching.

"Sorry, Miryam looked a little desperate there."

Jane grinned. Dawn bent down and pulled the playsuit in at the waist and began her process of pin gripping all the way around.

"This is a little baggy around the bum. I better take it in."

"That was really nice," commented Jane. "Helping the competition like that."

"We've all been there before," she said.

"It was still nice."

"A little birdy told me you're planning on retiring soon. Is it true?"

"Yeah, I don't want to outstay my welcome. I wanna explore myself a little more. You know what I mean?"

"Absolutely. Do you think you'll miss all this if you leave?"

"What, the last minute panics, bitchy competition and judgmental media? Hmmm."

"Oh, come on. There's more to it than all that and you know it."

"Yeah, I know. I'll miss the buzz of it all. I'll miss the money. And a lot of the friends I've made along the way, too. I'll miss the labels, being ahead of the fashion curve and, of course, the champagne."

Dawn laughed. "So, what will you do next?"

"I'm not sure. I don't have a plan exactly. My husband's a solicitor." She felt self-conscious suddenly, speaking about her husband to Dawn. It was like they were from different planets. "He's very career-minded," she stuttered. "I have enough savings to see me through, but I know I won't settle. I've thought about volunteering, I've got an interest in politics, maybe now I could even study some more."

"Well, that is a fantastic sign."

"What is?"

"You're already thinking what could be beyond all of

this," she said, waving her hands in the air. "You're seeing a future." She smiled enthusiastically and dropped the playsuit to Jane's feet.

"I suppose I am," she replied, lifting her toes out carefully.

"You know, I never realised you were married. How did I not know that?"

Jane looked surprised. "Yeah. Ten years. I'm just a really private person." She pulled at her leggings, then sat down, legs wide, t-shirt scrunched up in a ball between her hands. She stared into space. "I never thought I'd get so far, you know," she said, turning to look at Dawn. "I used to have so much self-doubt. I'd cry in the toilet every time I didn't get picked for a show. But you can't have them all, can ya? I know now, I suppose."

Dawn turned to face her. Jane's hair had fallen over her right eye.

"But now…"

"What?" Dawn asked, leaning forwards.

"I suppose I just thought we would reach the mountain top together, James and me. I fink naively, I believed that maybe we'd have a few kids by now, something to bond us together, you know what I mean?"

Dawn hung the dress and wrapped it, then held onto the playsuit. "Well, I have three kids, Jane, and it didn't stop my husband from sleeping with half of Leicester behind my back."

"Oh, I remember something about that splashed all over the papers. I'm so sorry, Dawn."

"I'm over it. To be honest, the romance was never really there for us." She stood with the playsuit under her folded arms. "We just kind of got on with each other. I was always at work, whilst he was always at home. The most it hurt was my ego."

"How old are your kids now?"

"My youngest boy is nine, then I have a son who is fifteen and a daughter who is sixteen."

"Sounds like a handful."

"I wouldn't know. I haven't spent enough time with any of them. They are wonderful human beings, but the credit must go to their dad. He's a fantastic father."

"What do they think of your career? The teens must love it."

"I think it's just part of life for them now. Each of the kids has been to fashion week at some point in their lives. My youngest, Troy, loves it and asks to come every year. Sometimes I take him. My PA Angie is good with him, she gets him doing fun activities whilst I'm busy. Actually, Troy would have been here this year, but he went away with the Scouts last week."

"It sounds to me like you don't give yourself enough credit, darlin'."

"Well… I don't know about that." She straightened and walked back a step. Terry walked in with a tray of coffee and croissants.

"Brekky time," he announced.

"Oh, no, not for me, Terry. I've already eaten more than I should have," Jane called back, holding her flat tummy like it was a watermelon.

"On this occasion, I'm afraid I must agree with Jane. I just finished fitting her, there's no room for fluctuations now."

# Nine

Jane showered and changed into fresh clothes. She straightened her hair and put serum on her face. Feeling strangely brighter, and a little peckish, she headed down the road to the shops.

On her return she saw the blue-haired woman, Gloria, hugging a child tightly, and she smiled. She headed for the studio, on her way in as Dawn's assistant was on the way out. She side-eyed her, her lip twitched.

"Hi, Jane."

She'd forgotten the woman's name. "Hey," she replied, catching the door.

Dawn was on the phone, facing the back window. It sounded as though the call was coming to an end, so Jane waited.

"That's wonderful! Give her a big hug from me. I know. Well…"

There was a moment of pause. "Okay, yep, love you too."

Jane passed Dawn one of the large bowls of salad she held in her hands.

Dawn said, "Oh, you angel, you brought lunch." Within seconds, was tearing off the lid and shovelling it into her mouth.

"Hungry, were ya?" Jane grinned.

"Yeah, I don't think I've eaten today."

Jane pushed a forkful of iceberg lettuce into her mouth, too. "Me neither. Was that your son on the phone?" she asked, holding the fork in front of her teeth.

"No, it was my ex-husband. He wanted to let me know that our daughter got a merit in her dance exams yesterday."

"Ah bless, you must be so proud of 'em."

"I am. I just hope she does so well in academic subjects."

"Well, if she's as smart as her mother, I'm sure she'll do fine."

Dawn gave a small shrug. "Oh, she's way smarter than me. She already gives me lectures about using fur and leather in my designs. She's a vegan, too. I honestly don't know where it comes from."

She dug into the centre of the salad bowl with her wooden fork to bring out the cous-cous.

"She just has no interest in maths or science."

"Maybe her strengths are in creative stuff 'n' all. Or maybe she will be an activist."

Dawn laughed. "Watch this space."

Jane held eye contact and grinned at her, and for a moment, she felt caught off guard. Was she showing too much interest in Dawn's personal life?

"You weren't joking about being on good terms with your ex, were you?"

"Oh, not at all. He's a lovely bloke. We just weren't meant to be," she answered, fork poised in front of her mouth. "Oh, my god, this is so good. At first, I thought, 'who puts fruit and roasted seeds in a salad?' But this is yum."

Jane chewed and swallowed. "Yep, I get one every time I come here. I love it."

Dawn watched her for a moment, admiring her firm body, her natural beauty, and the way her hair always fell over her left eye. The package made her almost untouchable, but she could see a vulnerability, in the way she talked when they were alone. And as she watched her eat her salad with such abandonment, it made her seem so human. Dawn wanted to know her better, to understand who she was beneath the façade. Suddenly, her mouth took action before her brain.

"Jane, hope you don't mind my asking. But do you know that you have a reputation for having no personality?"

Jane stopped chewing. "Subtle as ever, eh Dawny," she said, glancing around the room. "Of course, I know that. It's intentional 'n' all."

"Is it?"

"Yeah, it is. James, my husband, even nicknamed me Gizmo."

"Why Gizmo?"

"You know, not allowed out after nine, no champagne, that kind of thing."

"Like in the gremlins?" she asked, popping a cherry tomato into her mouth.

"The one and only."

"So, you've orchestrated the whole thing?"

"Damn right I have. Initially, it was to keep any negativity away from the media. Eventually, it became just a way of life."

"Is that healthy? Masking yourself from everyone. I'd imagine that would end in an eventual identity crisis."

Jane blinked. "It wasn't intentional to become a hidden person, but I can't see it affecting me like that. I'm already a very passive, shy, person, so it just fit."

"I see too many people in this industry being too perfect. What message is that sending to our future generations? Shouldn't you be standing up and showing them the real you? You're in a privileged position, and you're letting judgment win."

"Alright, don't get on your high horse. I get what you're saying. But, I mean, I don't think getting drunk and falling off of tables is particularly influential either, do you?"

"No, I know, bad behaviour isn't a healthy influence either. But I don't think you should be ashamed of who you are."

"What if the real me is a disaster?" She sighed. "Look, I'm not ashamed. I just don't know who I am, to know who to be, anymore."

"That can be quite powerful, you know."

"How?" she spluttered.

"When I was lost, I found myself through art and design. Some of my most loved dresses came from my darkest hours." She poked at a seed that was stuck between her teeth. "You hear it in all kinds of careers, too. Singers, poets, painters… the list goes on."

"Dawn, you're like a flipping guru sometimes, you know that?" She tossed her empty bowl into the bin.

Dawn felt her heart squeeze. She leant against the counter as Jane poured herself a glass of water. "And Jane, you're not hidden as well as you think you are. I already like you more than any other models I've ever worked with."

Jane looked over her glass, her eyebrows rose. "Why? I'm a flipping nightmare."

"Pah! I see through you."

Her lip wobbled. "You're not so bad yourself." She took a long gulp of water, then paused. "So, what was this deep, dark angst of yours that got your juices flowing?"

"Nothing and everything." Dawn sighed.

"Don't wanna talk about it?"

"It's not that. I just think it was to do with the divorce and the chance of losing my kids. Michael was their main carer; he was guaranteed to get full custody. And I was worried about his next move. It turned out, he wasn't going to turn into an enemy overnight, like I expected."

Dawn nodded solemnly.

***

Dawn rolled out a sheet of faux fur material so that Delvin was able to cut out a large section. His model stood behind him. She was dressed in a ripped-up denim jacket and fishnet stockings. He turned and pinned the faux fur around her waist, cutting it high up her thighs.

Jane laid back and stretched her arms up high, running her manicured nails around the fur beneath her.

"Thanks, Dawn," said Delvin. She placed her hands on her hips and watched him walk away.

"No problem," she called after him.

She collapsed into a heap beside Jane with a *guwaff*, and for a moment they lay in cosy silence, the chatters and laughter and screams of a busy study filling the air.

"What are your plans after this show?" Jane asked her.

Dawn combed both hands through the front of her hair. "In terms of the label, you mean?"

"I actually mean more personally."

"Well, I suppose work is my personal life lately. It has been for a while now. To be honest, some of the designers I started out with are only just being taken seriously as designers now. But I don't think I'll continue designing clothes forever. I want to spend some time with my kids before I miss it all, maybe travel a bit."

"That sounds ideal." Jane spun around onto her tummy and rested her chin in her hands. "I've always wanted to see a bit more of the world."

"You must have travelled though?" Dawn asked.

"I s'pose. I mean, you could say I've been all over the world. But hotel rooms, concert halls and most airports are pretty much the same no matter where in the world you are."

"What a good point. I know exactly what you mean. I've somewhat travelled for work; you don't get to take in the culture or experience the lifestyle at all, do you?"

"Exactly, babe, you must do the same, mustn't you?"

"I mean, we've also been camping and stuff occasionally with the kids. But I get what you mean. I've always dreamed of sitting in a Parisian café with a coffee or drinking champagne in one of those hip little bars by the river."

"Eating baguettes or frogs' legs by the Eiffel Tower?" She giggled.

"Well, all but the frogs' legs," Dawn replied, screwing up her face.

"All part of the culture though, init."

"I'm sure it isn't in this day and age."

"Okay, maybe it's not common anymore. But it's a delicacy, eh? So, it might be worth a try."

Dawn lifted onto her elbows and raised an eyebrow. "Well, we are here in Paris until morning. Maybe we should get out whilst we can, maybe we should celebrate completing the outfits."

"And here's me thinking you were sensible."

"You mean boring, don't you?"

"A little." She laughed.

"Well, you're right, but it doesn't hurt to let off some steam now and then, does it?"

Jane laughed. "That's true, and my reputation's probably already ruined by now, what wiv Marilyn and her blooming camera crew. Let's get one thing straight, I won't be dancing naked on the Eiffel Tower or having a one-night stand, mind you. Maybe we could drink a little coffee in one of those Paris cafés, try a cocktail at one of those hip little bars you're on about. Or even try a piece of French baguette?" she said, with a wink.

"Wow, those papers really do have you wrong. Where's Charlie when you need him?" she said, looking around the room.

Jane began to laugh. "Stop. I keep losing the nerve. If you wanna go, we better do it now, whilst I'm feeling brave."

"In that case, let's get out of here."

# Ten

Dawn stepped out of the shower. She pulled on the black dress with several puffy layers of skirt and stepped into a pair of strappy black kitten heels that she always put in her case for emergencies. She dusted a natural bronzing powder over her face with just a touch of eyeliner. Then straightened her hair. She wondered what Jane would wear. Would she dress-up, or down to be discrete? She looked in the mirror, thinking she looked half decent, a warm glow of excitement tinted her cheeks just right.

There was a tap at the door. She glanced at her watch before reaching for the door handle. But when she opened it, it was Terry who was staring back at her, a bulging plastic carrier bag in his hand.

"Terry?" she asked in surprise.

He blinked nervously. "Sorry. Ahh." He pressed his free fist into his lips. "I'm such an idiot."

She squinted at him, and he looked up in defeat.

"I assumed you wouldn't have eaten. So, I brought you dinner." He rolled his eyes and shrugged his shoulders.

“Coq au Vin and French bread,” he announced, raising the bag.

“Oh, Terry,” she murmured.

“But you’re otherwise engaged. Of course, you bloody well are, a beautiful, fascinating, woman like you. Like you’d just be sitting around all alone in your hotel room in one of the most romantic cities in the world.”

“It’s okay, I often do just that.”

He looked her up and down. “You scrub up well, by the way.”

She laughed.

“I mean, you look absolutely bloody stunning, woman,” he said with a grin.

“Thank you.” She blushed. “And it was so thoughtful of you to bring me food,” she said, suggesting towards the bag that was now stretching in his left hand.

“I will let you go,” he said with a smile, meeting her eye before turning on his heel. “He’s a lucky guy, whoever he is,” he threw back. She smiled, watching him walk away, thinking what a sweet man he was. She knew she’d allowed him to think she was going on a date. But no matter how nice he was, Terry was a journalist, and she knew that he wouldn’t think twice about stabbing either of them in the back for a scoop. She wasn’t about to let that happen. They needed this.

They met back in Jane’s room once they were both ready. Jane was wearing a layered pink dress with a darker pink Kaftan and flat shoes. She had on a wig of long blonde hair.

“Wow, Jane, that hair makes you look like a completely different person.”

"That's the idea," she said.

"Sensible option on the shoes, too. I looked out of the window earlier and thought even these tiny heels are potential ankle breakers on those cobbled roads."

"It's okay. We can take the left pavement all the way, if you prefer."

"It doesn't matter to me, I'll survive."

"Brave woman. You ready to go?"

"I am. I should warn you, though, I'm old now and therefore will probably be ready for bed by nine."

Jane laughed. "See, we aren't so different after all. And besides," she said with a wink, "I saw you pull an all-nighter last night."

Dawn put her hand to her tummy as it whirled out of control. It had been a long time since she'd gone 'out, out', but it wasn't just that that was making her nervous. The way that Jane was watching her lips as she spoke, felt strangely intimate. But she hadn't expected butterflies in her tummy or the nerves that were tingling up her ribs. It looked as though Jane wanted to kiss her, and rather than feel terrified, she felt hopeful. But of what, she wasn't sure.

They stepped out of the clean, bright lobby and into the chilly, dull evening on the Parisian streets.

"It's chucking it down," moaned Dawn.

Jane turned back and grabbed an umbrella from a bucket in the lobby. They ran over the road together, heading for the shelter of a tree whilst attempting to tip toe over the cobbles. Jane pulled open the umbrella, and with a chuckle they huddled underneath.

It was a small, narrow road, unsuitable for cars. Each house possessed rows of hanging baskets full of a variety of colourful flowers. The top of the street opened up to the wider, busier streets, and as they moved closer to the city, Dawn thought she could smell the sweetness of pastries blended with the nutty smell of coffee that awakened her senses. The rain pattered out and when they turned the corner, the Eiffel Tower stood proud, its lights glistening in the river Seine. They walked over the bridge, the reflection of the lights twinkling in the water below as it rocked back and forth.

Dawn stopped and inhaled deeply, admiring the beauty of it. When she turned, she saw Jane watching her. She rubbed her hands together.

"What?"

Jane blinked slowly. "It's a beautiful thing. To witness another person's awe."

"I've just never seen the Eiffel Tower up close like this before."

"Never?"

"Never."

"You would love the view from the top. Shall we see how big the queue is?"

Dawn nodded, feeling the nerves of a teenage girl as they arose again. She huddled under the umbrella close to Jane as they walked over the bridge.

"So, you said you don't go out much anymore? What do you do when you're not working?"

"I usually cook with my kids. Sometimes we go on nature walks together and find leaves and rocks to paint, sometimes we make a cinema in the lounge and watch a kids' movie."

"You sound like a fun mum."

"Not always. Sometimes they don't want to be around me. And for those nights I have a little studio bedroom where I draw up new ideas for my collection. And drink wine from a tiny pink beaker," she said with a grin.

"I'm sorry that your husband cheated on you," she whispered. "For the record, he must be a complete idiot."

"He's a nice guy, we just weren't right for each other."

"Was it hard finding out?"

"No, but it didn't help that his indiscretions were so public."

"Honestly, the media are scum. I may keep out of the limelight, but sometimes they print stuff anyway. And it angers me."

"The media can be good and bad. And if you're not being talked about, then no-one cares enough."

"Let them not care."

"You really aren't a public person, are you?"

"No, and I have no idea why you would be either, if they embarrassed you the way you say they did."

Dawn grabbed Jane by the wrist and yanked her over the gap in the busy road. The wind blew against them.

"I didn't say they embarrassed me. They just took full advantage of sharing pictures of my husband cheating. And why wouldn't they? It's human interest."

Jane stopped on the pavement and turned to face Dawn. "And that doesn't infuriate you?"

"Of course, it infuriated me. But it wasn't the journalists that cheated on me. I hated Michael at the time."

"And now you're clearly amicable from what I heard earlier..."

"Yes, we are."

"You're a very forgiving person, Dawn Lewis."

"I don't think I am particularly, but why would I hold on to that anger? He only cheated because something inside wasn't fulfilling him. He just realised before I did because he was the one at home, waiting for me all the time."

"Was she the only one?"

"Oh, no, there were around six. That I knew of. But when he met the one, he left me, they ended up together. And he has been brilliant with our kids. She is, in fact, brilliant with our kids. I can't complain."

Jane's eyes widened. "Wow."

"Why's it such a shock? Honestly, if you were unhappy in your marriage and felt happier once you were apart, then you too would feel this sense of calm."

Jane gulped and looked up at Dawn through her thick lashes. "But how did you know you weren't happy?"

Dawn looked back at her. "Honestly? I didn't. Not really. After he left me, and life started to settle, I had an evening all to myself. I made myself a slap-up meal, had a bubble bath and I fell asleep watching a movie. And when I woke up, the next morning, I stretched out under the sheets, and I realised something. I hadn't woken at 5am with the sense of dread or guilt that I'd been feeling every morning for several years."

Jane blinked. "You felt guilty because you didn't love him?"

"I must have."

"And you aren't looking for anyone else?"

"I'm enjoying the time I have, working and spending spare time with my kids. Sometimes I fantasise about some faceless person. In my images, they're usually jogging beside me on a beach or lake. Maybe sitting at a restaurant eating seafood or pasta. We're laughing at each other and drinking red wine. Or sometimes we're just cuddled up in front of a crackling fireplace, watching a movie."

"They're very specific scenarios."

"Yeah, I suppose they're just the things I never did with Michael. I always felt boring with him. Like I was holding him back."

"But you're the most interesting person I've met in a long time."

"I appreciate that, but I'm often the quietest person in the room. Happy just being."

"I like that quality. Maybe it's the reason I find you so calming to be around."

"It's also the reason I made excuses for Michael's cheating for so long."

"That's a lot of responsibility to take on."

"It didn't bother me. Well, not until people started giving me that sympathetic look. Like I was some kind of victim. Then when he was spotted with the same woman several times, I knew it was leave or be left. So, I left."

"And you didn't regret it?"

"The only thing I regretted was that I hadn't done it sooner. You probably have no idea what I'm talking about, because what kind of crazy man would ever cheat on you?"

"I suppose any man or woman can cheat. But I don't think I'd take it so calmly. I'd have to get revenge, whether I loved him or not."

Dawn laughed at that. "That's just your ego talking."

"I just hate the idea of someone taking me for a fool."

"It's not always about that. I think Michael was genuinely torn."

They approached the Eiffel Tower. "Like I say, you're a better woman than me."

After paying, they stood in the small queue.

"What's your husband like?"

"He's driven."

"I mean, what kind of husband is he?"

They stepped forwards with the queue. Dawn could feel the cold settling in her bones. Jane squinted her eyes in contemplation. Then looked at Dawn.

"I don't even know who he is. Don't you ever get that feeling? Like, you can spend every evening lying beside someone in bed, without really knowing what's going through their mind. Or even what their likes or dislikes are."

Dawn gulped. "Yeah, I do. My husband had a whole other life. But James isn't cheating on you. Maybe now that you're considering retirement, you can get to know each other all over again. It could have the excitement of a new relationship."

"Maybe," she said, climbing ahead of Dawn, looking away.

They got to the second floor. The cold, wet rain was slamming into her face like ice, and she understood why people weren't queuing much to get up there. The railing was damp and slippery to the touch. She felt a fear of heights as she caught sight of the gaps between each step. They reached another level and stepped onto the platform; she looked up at the city of Paris in full view, all sprinkled with lights through the evening sky. The damp wind didn't seem so bad on the platform. She took in a breath, filling her lungs, and turned to look at Jane. She wished in that moment that she had a camera with her. Jane looked breathtaking. She was standing against the railings, the night sky illuminated behind her, her pink dress and fake blonde hair floating around in the wind. Her eyes glistening.

Jane walked over to her and peered over the edge. She gulped in the cold air.

"Have you ever seen anything this spectacular?"

Jane turned and they locked eyes. "Breathtaking," she replied, then she cleared her throat and headed back towards the steps.

"You know, you're accent sounds kind of northern," Dawn commented.

They ascended the steps.

"No, it's not!" She laughed. "I'm south London through and through!"

"I was under the impression your mum grew up on a council estate, somewhere up-north."

"I see, so you were fishing, were ya?" She smirked. "Mum's originally from Nottingham. She moved to London once she started modelling."

"Brave"

"She's always been ambitious. I'll give her that."

After making their way back down the stairs, they had a coffee outside the river Seine and walked the damp, moonlit streets of Paris. They brought a baguette and shared it as they meandered along, ripping off thumb sized pieces.

"I keep thinking Charlie's going to be hiding in a bush somewhere." Dawn laughed.

"Yeah, I can just imagine that in tomorrow's rag. Us two on the streets of Paris, a pair of drowned rats, stuffing bread into our mouths."

"Me too. Only, knowing my luck, I'd be mid-open-mouthed chew whilst you'd be looking all elegant with your tiny piece of bread held out in front of you."

Jane snorted at that.

"All of the time I've spent in this city, and I never got to see it like this before."

Dawn said, "Me neither. But I suppose that's why we're both successful women. How many fashion weeks have you actually been to?"

"Well, let's see... eight different shows a year since I was about ten years old."

Dawn followed her eyes and smirked. She was looking at the sky as she calculated.

"What's that, about 280?"

"It's a lot. You've always gone to them all twice a year?"

"Mostly. I missed one when I was projectile vomiting as a child. Aside from that, I'd go with any other ailment. I had to take my schoolwork and a tutor along with me half of the time, too. My mum didn't trust anyone else to look after me. So, if I didn't go, she didn't go. And the limelight was the only one thing she loved more than me."

"Wow, my clothing range didn't even get into a show until I was twenty-six, and I don't always get into the New York shows, even now. But I've been to a fair few of the others."

"So, you've been going for, what, fifteen years?"

"Nearer twenty."

"You know, we may have met before," Jane said, popping a rolled-up piece of bread onto the end of her tongue.

"We might have even spoken to each other. Have you ever worn me?"

Jane smiled at that. "I didn't even know your label until a couple of years ago. They gave me your strappy platform to wear with a Gucci dress in Milan in spring. I remember because they were so comfortable, they had this spongy effect."

"Ahhh, the Conthia's, I suspect."

"That sounds right, yeah."

"Yes, I designed them when the papers were showing Michael cheek to cheek with his now wife, Leslie. I knew in that moment they had something special. I went to my studio and thought, 'I'm going to create something that will not only make a woman look good, but it will bring her comfort too.'"

"Only you could think of ways to help others in the midst of your own pain."

"It's not like I went to a homeless shelter or anything. My company made a huge profit on those shoes."

"Still."

"So, you have worn my label. I'm glad. Was it an exciting childhood for you, all of those shows?"

Jane paused, she had been asked this question many times before and she'd always just smiled and agreed – the motto was always to answer giving nothing away. But she felt like she could be honest with Dawn.

"It was, but it also made me socially awkward. People would praise my mum or try to make friends with me to get to her, so I didn't form many genuine friendships. And my mum always had a lot of different boyfriends 'n' all. I suppose I just never really felt good enough, living in her shadow. God, I just heard myself, uh that's gross. I sound privileged as shit, don't I?"

"No, you don't. To me, you sound human. Jane, you are such a genuine person, you're not fighting for attention, or cat fighting other models you feel threatened by. I've seen you encourage other models. So, you obviously grew somewhere along the line. And, I mean, you're in a long-term relationship with your husband. So, you aren't following her in that sense."

She hesitated. "Hmmm."

"I know you said you felt a little distant from your husband. But marriages have difficulties, don't they? Do you think you two will get past it?"

In the back of her mind, Dawn selfishly hoped that Jane's relationship wouldn't work, but guilt quickly squashed the feeling.

"I don't know," Jane said. "I don't even know if I want to make it through. It's sort of non-existent... if you know what I mean?"

"I know what you mean," Dawn whispered.

She glanced at a bar over the road. People in their twenties and thirties were spilling from the doors with cocktails in their hands. She watched as they laughed and joked. A woman placed her hand on the chest of a man, bent her leg behind her, tapping her toe to the curb whilst smiling flirtatiously.

Jane followed her eyes. "You either fancy a cocktail, the man or... the woman?" she remarked with a grin.

"Sorry, I'm staring, aren't I? I always do it, it used to get me in trouble when I was younger. They just look like they're having so much fun. I wouldn't say no to a cocktail, though. What do you think, hip enough for you?"

"It'll do."

They headed across the street, Dawn throwing well over half of the remaining baguette into a bin as they passed by.

***

Inside the 'Club de Rue' was a fountain of Champagne – they brought an empty glass each and a man filled it up from the stream.

After the champagne, Dawn slipped into a small gap at the bar to order two cocktails. She looked around at all the people waiting hunched around the bar. She hadn't missed this, the uncertainty of knowing when it was your turn, not wanting to be pushed to the back, or push in front of someone.

A woman approached the bar beside her. She was short with tight curled blonde hair. She whined at the man by her side that her feet ached, with an American drawl typical of those on the east coast. She turned to Dawn.

"Quite the queue, right?"

Dawn smiled and nodded.

"American?" she asked.

"English," Dawn replied, stretching her neck over the bar.

"Ahh, I see. What do you think about Jeffrey Archer going down?" the woman asked.

Dawn glanced at her curiously, then back to the barman, who gave her a finger in recognition.

"I don't really have an opinion about it, to be honest," she replied, nodding back to him.

"Ahh, I see, never been into his books?"

"Never read them."

"Looks like the bartender spotted ya," she said, nodding towards the barman. "We've just been to the club across the road. Couldn't get service in there at all."

"Well, I suspect a few people wanted to relax after fashion week."

"Of course." The man put his hands on the woman's shoulders.

"So, what brings you here from England?" she asked.

"Fashion week," she answered, no longer looking at them.

The woman didn't seem to get the message. "I see. Well, we're looking for a bit of adventure," she said pointedly.

"Oh?" she asked, distracted.

"Yeah, it's my husband's thirtieth birthday, you see, and I kinda wanted to treat him."

"Well, they say that Paris is the place for romance and adventure."

The barman was putting the last drinks through the till as someone at the bar leant closer to him and stuck a note in the air. She was getting irritated.

"Right. So, I've heard," the woman purred.

Dawn leant over further, trying to maintain the barman's attention.

"Well, I'm Amber and this is my husband, Cory. Can we buy you a drink?"

She caught his eye, and glanced back over the crowded room at Jane, who was watching the bar too. Without looking back at the woman, she answered, "Oh, no, that's okay, thank you. I'm having drinks with my friend over there."

They glanced over at the table and Amber's eyes widened. "Wow, she looks so much like that famous model. Doesn't she look like that model, Cory?"

Cory shrugged.

"You know, the one who was sleeping with Robbie Williams."

"Ahhh yeah, Marietta something or other," he said. "The one who did that video with all the bending and stretching." His eyes glazed over, and Amber nudged him in his rounded belly.

"That's it," she exclaimed. "Marietta George."

Finally, the barman was on his way over to her, ignoring the note being waved in front of him.

"Yeah, she gets told that a lot," Dawn replied absently, smiling at the barman.

"Well, we will leave you to your date then. Sorry, we thought you were here alone."

"Oh, no problem," Dawn said, leaning in so that she could order from the barman.

When she turned back round, the annoying couple were still standing there. The woman leant in closer, speaking in a subtle voice.

"In case we weren't clear before, we were looking for a third party to add to our little party tonight, you see, and, well, Cory here, he saw you from the other side of the room and I just wanted to… erm, treat him."

Dawn coughed into her hand in an attempt to hide the horrified laugher that escaped her lips. She paid the barman and took her drinks, giving the couple a gracious smile.

"Well, got to go, thanks though," she said, her voice sounding strangely high pitched.

She moved away as quickly as she could. They moved into the gap and watched her walk away, puzzlement on their faces. Dawn knew it had been a while since she'd been on the bar scene, but is this what people did now? Asked random strangers for threesomes? She walked to the table where Jane was sitting and placed down two Cosmopolitans.

"Hitting on ya, were they?" Jane asked over her glass.

Dawn gave her a look of surprise. "How did you know?"

"I saw them checking you out before subtly standing next to you and making conversation. Don't tell me, a woman wants to treat hubby with a threesome?"

"How could you possibly know that?"

"It's a thing."

"It is not a thing."

"It is, even I know that, and I don't go anywhere."

Dawn looked gobsmacked, then took a sip of her drink. "Wait, if you saw it, why didn't you come and save me?"

Jane laughed. "What, and take away the fun of watching you squirm whilst politely turning them down?"

Dawn gave her an incredulous look. "They thought we were on a date. I didn't correct them. I thought it would be a nicer way to let them down."

Jane grinned. "I don't have a problem with that. You can be my date any time."

Dawn felt herself heating from the inside out.

***

"Did you always want to be a model?"

"Not always. Growing up, I wanted to be a veterinary nurse, then as I got good at gymnastics, I saw a future there."

"And you were in competitions?"

"No, not really. I was invited to compete in the London nationals, but I couldn't go. We were always in different cities for mum's career. And she didn't like leaving me with anyone, so I was forced to quit classes, eventually. After that, I grovelled until I got a personal trainer, Trevor, his name was. He came round with me. Must have cost Mum a small fortune. But it wasn't the same without my teammates, so I fired him after a few months."

"That must have been annoying."

"I s'pose, but Mum made it possible for me to have everything I needed, and she did so without dumping me off on anyone."

"Parents with demanding careers are never easy on their kids." She sighed.

Jane turned to her then, sympathetically. "Oh, gosh. Please don't take that personally, Dawny. You're there for your kids, and they also have a perfectly good father."

"I am lucky. Michael is very supportive. Have you never been curious about your own father?"

"No, Mum never knew who he was, and it was always me and her. He's a stranger who I don't care about, but all the upheaval in her life and mine gives me a craving for stability and normality now," she mused.

"I can imagine, god. I was in my twenties when I started all of this, and it seemed like a massive upheaval."

"It was different, but I always had that stability off me mum. Plus, it gave me a massive advantage knowing the practice inside-out. You grew up in Leicester, didn't you?"

"I did. My parents are from a small village to the south."

Dawn spoke about having Saturday night game night with her family of six, she spoke about pie baking on a Sunday and how they all chipped in with the chores, moaning and whining as they polished and hoovered and did a bit of washing. She spoke about how summer Sunday afternoons were often spent with the wider family, playing cricket on the park. Then she admitted, for the first time, how guilty she felt that her parents were ageing, and she had been too busy for them. That her brothers and sisters had invited her to family gatherings and that she had, more often than not, turned them down.

Dawn realised how relaxed they'd both become in each other's company. Like long-lost family or friends reunited. They laughed with strangers from different countries around the world. They danced to a couple of their favourite songs, they joked and talked and drank until Jane was slurring and Dawn was swaying, and they decided it was time to call it a night.

They stepped outside, huddling together against the cold chill in the air.

"What do you think of Paris now you've actually seen it then?" Jane asked, stopping to pull on her pump that had come loose. She straightened. Their eyes locked a moment longer than necessary, and Dawn breathed in the scent of Paris.

"Almost like I don't want to go home," Dawn replied honestly, then she leant back in and grabbed Jane's arm.

"Well, maybe tomorrow we can do the same fing all over again, in Vegas," she laughed.

***

They walked along the quiet streets in a comfortable silence, beneath the flashing lights that were woven through the trees.

"This must be what people at home picture me doing when I have to travel all over the world. In reality, all I see are studios and hotel rooms, and mostly I just want to get back to my kids."

"I can imagine. God, if I had kids to go home to, I wouldn't want to be watching yet another fashion show, measuring another moody model or smiling for the cameras either."

"The models aren't all bad. You said before that you imagined yourself having kids. Is that something you're planning for the future?"

"Nah, not really. James don't want kids. He says they'd hold us back." She paused. "Although, sometimes it feels like we're staying together for the sake of not breaking up."

Dawn didn't reply, she waited, as though knowing Jane hadn't worked through the thoughts in her mind.

"Did your kids take your break-up hard?"

Dawn pondered the question. "My youngest a little,

but they seemed to bounce back. Jane, if you aren't happy, then why do you stay together?"

"So far, it's been for convenience, I s'pose, more than anything. Now I'm gonna be retired, I'm reconsidering things. But I don't have an actual reason to leave him."

"Not being compatible is reason enough. What drew you to him in the first place?"

She stood pondering on the question. "His ambition, his love of life. But that was a long time ago. Now it's different. Now I have different priorities. He's different 'n' all."

"Sounds like you've already made your mind up."

"S'pose, I dunno." she replied, looking down at her shoes.

"I think reaching your forties makes you realise how quickly the years pass by. Maybe you should bear that in mind."

"And nights like tonight make me realise what I am missing out on. God, where did my twenties even go?" She sighed.

"Well, let's see, you aced modelling for a start, then you got married and, I suspect, bought a house?"

Jane nodded and rolled her eyes. "I know, I just never did… this kind of stuff."

"All I'm saying is, don't ever overlook your accomplishments. You made those sacrifices for your successes, you've earnt it."

"I s'pose. I'm just scared. You said earlier I could have an identity crisis. What if I have one from leaving everything that 'makes me' behind?"

"You won't. You'll realise there's more to you than your career and the person you've chosen as a partner."

"I don't think there's much more to me than that to be fair."

"Rubbish! It's the 'more to you' that's outgrown this life. This is just you shedding a shell."

She inhaled deeply. "I hope you're right."

They looked at each other and sniggered.

"If all else fails, you can always come back to Paris to dance and drink."

"I do love Paris. But it's you that I feel I've missed out on, Dawn."

"Missed out on me? You never met me," said Dawn.

"But I feel like I should have known you," she whispered in response.

Dawn gulped. She wanted to respond, but no words felt right.

Jane rubbed her hands together. "It's getting cold now, init? Shall we get moving?"

"Let's, my arse cheeks are freezing."

They both laughed as they made their way back to the hotel. The streets were calm and peaceful, they walked in silence, but Jane's words were lodged in her throat like apple.

"It's so nice not to be bothered by photographers," said Jane eventually. She stretched out her arms.

"Have they not yet discovered that we haven't all left?"

"Oh no, they'd have been tipped off about the Vegas show, probably before we even knew about it. They're still here alright."

"You think the wig worked?" asked Dawn.

"I doubt it, they're probably off chasing the young and hip models. Fortunately, I am no longer either."

"Does that annoy you?"

"No, it's a relief."

"But it bothers you a little bit."

"Nah."

"Come on, you can tell me the truth…"

"How do you do that? Not even my own mother could read me."

"I don't think it's me doing it, I think it's you thawing out."

Jane pulled a face of mock horror.

"So come on, what worries you about ageing?"

"It's not ageing, per say. But I always hated journalists. They wouldn't leave me alone; they imprisoned me, to a certain extent. But they sort of played a role in my identity from birth. So, part of me doesn't like the change. It's another sign that I'm no longer desirable."

"Sounds like Stockholm syndrome to me," Dawn said sarcastically.

Jane laughed sadly.

"Oh Jane, wait until they see you in that dress tomorrow. They'll soon be pissing you off again; chasing you down the road, sitting outside your house, frequenting your favourite restaurants," Dawn said with a wink. Jane side-eyed her.

They stepped into the hotel lobby.

"Fancy a cup of tea? Get your hands warmed up before bed?"

Dawn knew she shouldn't, she was exhausted and had only hours before they had to set off again. But she didn't want the night to end.

"Go on then, just a quick cuppa."

***

They sat on the huge bed with their oversized cups of tea. Jane placed her mug on the bedside cabinet, and laid upside down with her feet against the headboard.

"Isn't it strange that we only just met. I feel like I've known you forever."

"I was thinking the same thing earlier," Dawn said, crossing her legs, hugging a pillow to her chest. "Some people you meet can be perfectly nice, yet you just don't connect with them. Others you slowly build a relationship with, then occasionally you meet someone… they can even behave like a total bitch when you meet them…" she said with a laugh.

Jane looked up and grinned at the cheeky glint in Dawn's eye.

"And yet," she intentionally strung out her sentence. Speaking slowly, she continued, "it feels like you were meant to meet them. Almost like your souls already knew each other. What is that?"

"I have no idea," Jane said, pulling a pack of cigarettes from her purse, opening them and placing one in between her lips. "But I bet there's a name for it. Something like, *ignis kismet*," she said, her voice muffled through the cigarette.

"False karma," Dawn suggested.

Jane inhaled deeply, blowing smoke into the air. "Advantageous serendipity," she announced.

"I like that one… advantageous serendipity." Dawn giggled.

"Yeah, I don't think it's anything to do with souls reuniting, though."

"No, me neither. But it does now."

"Alright, we're redefining it's meaning." Jane laughed.

"Deal. Hey, I didn't know you smoked."

"Only occasionally, only in private."

"They will kill you."

"Not if I die from boredom first."

"Don't be so morbid and give us a drag," she said, watching her inhale with a look of satisfaction.

"Nope. You don't smoke."

"Neither do you."

She laid down, her head by Jane's. Her legs hanging over the opposite end of the bed. Jane shrugged and passed the cigarette over, watching as she blew out a large cloud above them.

"Look at us, coming to Paris fashion week, sneaking out, going to bars and smoking a cigarette. We're such rebels."

"Hardly. It's 12.30pm on a Saturday night and we're back in your room with a cup of tea."

"Total rock stars." Jane nodded, making the goose down feather crinkle beneath her head.

"Total." Dawn snorted, passing back the cigarette back, feeling her head haze as though she'd just taken a drag of weed. "I suppose we ought to get packed soon, don't we leave at 4.30am?"

They turned to each other and groaned simultaneously.

"I don't want to get up."

"Me neither," she said, her breath catching in her throat.

As they lay chatting, Dawn found herself telling Jane all about her kids.

"I love how much you appreciate them. I never got to be a mum, and I hate to see when people have kids but don't appreciate them."

"I'm sorry. It was selfish of me boasting about them, when you've already told me you'd like to have been a mum. But you're not too old, you know, if that is what you want."

"Don't feel bad, I already told you I like to hear it. And I would, but I would need to find a willing father first, one who isn't my husband."

"Well, there are other ways. I sometimes think about fostering when I get older, it would be nice to help kids who need a place."

Jane docked her cigarette out into an old cardboard coffee cup, which was laid out on the bedside cabinet. Then she spun over. She put her chin into the palms of her hands.

"That's beautiful. Maybe one day we could buy a big house together, me and you. Then we could foster loads of kids."

Dawn laughed out loud, an image of them running around in a large farmhouse with kids and dogs and an enormous Christmas tree.

"Are your kids interested in design, too?"

"No. My nine-year-old son wants to be something different week by week, my fifteen-year-old son wants to be a spinal surgeon and my sixteen -year-old daughter wants to study English Literature at university."

"Wow, quite the combination."

"And… here I am, talking about my kids again."

She sat up and swung around, crossing her legs to face Jane.

Jane looked at her. "You should never apologise for

that," she said, picking up her mug of tea from the bedside cabinet. She sipped at it.

"It's funny, isn't it? Two successful women, and the one thing neither of us have figured out is love… the most natural thing in the world, apparently," Dawn said with a smile.

"You're right. Maybe that's the problem. Women are tearing themselves apart to have a career, to be beautiful, to be a good mother and a good wife. It's a juggle."

"We will figure it out."

"I just fear I may be on my deathbed when I get that revelation." Laughed Jane.

"Don't be silly. Anyway, it's getting late. I can see your eyes drifting. I'm going back to my room to get a couple of hours shut eye before the craziness begins once more." Dawn stood and Jane followed her towards the door.

"Yeah, you're right. Dawn, thank you for tonight. It was just what I needed."

Dawn stopped at the door and turned to face her. She felt her stomach whirl. "Me too," she said quietly.

They locked eyes. Dawn's eyes travelled over her lips and they both seemed to lean into each other. Then, without another word, Dawn turned on her heel and walked away.

Jane watched her walk away, down the corridor. She shut and locked the door and slipped under the sheets. It had been a long time since she'd connected with anyone like that. She felt the most content she had in a while. She set her alarm and switched off the lamp. But rather than fall off to sleep, she replayed the night over and over in her mind.

Little did she know that Dawn was in her own room doing the exact same thing.

# Eleven

There was a low mist hovering over the city. The trees waved along with the slow rhythmic wind. Dawn zipped up her luggage and popped two paracetamols into her mouth, washing them down with a bottle of leftover sparkling Perrier water. Her head hurt; she knew there was a reason she'd stopped drinking more than two drinks at a time by the age of thirty. She pulled on her white training shoes and ran down to the studio. People were already wrapped up and ready to go, and so she quickly hung her designs inside the hanging rail that was about to be zipped up and flown to Las Vegas. Terry was sitting by the sewing machine with a cup of coffee in his hand.

"Woo-hoo. Looks like you had a heavy night. Did you have fun?" he asked, looking at her dubiously.

"Yes, my head hurts. But it was amazing, actually." She smiled as she said it. "But listen, Terry, I—"

He cut her off. "It's fine, honestly." He grinned. "I didn't really expect you to go out with me. But you can't blame a guy for trying, eh?"

She smiled and put a hand on his shoulder. He passed his half drank cup of coffee to her. She took it gratefully and drank. It was hot and strong. She hummed in pleasure as it went down.

"Paperwork complete?" he asked.

"I didn't get a chance."

"I'll help you if you like, on the plane," he offered, taking his empty mug back from her and peering into it.

"Okay… I appreciate that, thanks. Have you seen Jane this morning?"

"I think she went to speak to the make-up ladies or something. She's travelling with them down to the airport. We might as well get one car together, hadn't we? That way, I can ask you a few questions along the way."

"Okay, great," she said, trying to hide the stab of disappointment.

Once her bags were at the door and they safely carted her designs off, she took a moment to call and check in on her kids. She grabbed herself a banana and a black coffee from her room and headed for reception.

As she went out to the car, she spotted Jane with a group of other women. She ignored the feeling of rejection tugging at her. Jane was wearing a pair of white skinny jeans, with loafers and a tank top. Her hair was slapped back into a tight ponytail, and she had on thick black eyeliner that went out in a flick. Dawn thought how beautiful and fresh-faced she looked, especially for someone who must have only slept a few hours. Terry approached. He regarded her.

"Admiring Jane again?" he asked.

"I was just thinking how fresh-faced she looks so early in the morning."

"Well, maybe she had an early night," he hissed.

Gloria and her daughter approached. "Hey, Dawn."

"Hey, Gloria. How are you both getting on?"

"Fantastic. It's been great having Lucy here. Thank you so much for your help."

Dawn shrugged it off and looked down at the little girl. "Are you enjoying watching Mummy hard at work, Lucy?" she asked.

"She doesn't do a lot, but the ladies look very pretty. I want to make dresses when I grow up, too."

"Aren't you a sweetheart?" said Terry, a big smile on his face. "Did you like the plane ride here?"

She nodded shyly.

"Are you both going to Vegas?" Dawn asked.

"We are. Lucy had never travelled on a plane, now it's twice in one week."

"Have you heard from the ex?" Dawn whispered.

"Not a thing. But I've been in touch with a solicitor."

Dawn rubbed her arm. "Good. Good for you."

"Listen, I'd better go and make sure we have everything, but I just wanted to introduce the two of you."

"I appreciate that, Gloria." She raised her voice an octave. "Nice to meet you, young lady."

"Nice to meet you, too."

As she waved them off, her eyes found Jane once more. Jane glanced back. On seeing Dawn, her eyes lit up and she smiled, filling Dawn's stomach with butterflies. She made her excuse to the women she was talking to and walked straight over.

"Hey, how are you feeling this morning?"

"Good thanks, the tiredness must have not yet caught

up with me. What about you?"

She saw Terry give her a look of indignation from the corner of her eye.

"I'm good. I requested a table on the plane so that we can finish up the paperwork."

"Okay, great."

"How are you today, Terry?"

"Very well, thank you. I'm looking forward to seeing Sean Combs again. I interviewed him a couple of months back, he's a stand-up guy."

"Yes, Troy is going to die when I tell him he missed P. Diddy."

"He's a fan?" asked Jane.

"Yep, he loves him. The kids have all met a few celebrities at these events, but he is Troy's favourite."

"Awh, what a shame he isn't here."

"It is."

"Wanna join us in the car, Dawny?"

"Oh, it's okay, thanks. I've already got one booked with Terry and Angie."

"In that case, I should come with you guys." She turned before Dawn could respond and had gone to speak to the crowd she had come in with. A few minutes later, she was back.

Terry leant into Dawn's ear.

"Well, she has certainly done a 180. What did I miss?"

Dawn flinched. "What do you mean? Nothing. Why?"

He gave her a sarcastic smile. "There's something you aren't telling me, Lewis."

"No, there isn't. She was just a bit jet lagged when we got here, that was all."

"Jet lagged? From London to Paris? Pah. Don't talk rubbish."

"That happens. People get jet lagged."

He side-eyed her as Jane reappeared.

"Well, at least once the paperwork's sorted, we might actually get a bit of shut-eye on the plane, eh?" she said, looking from Terry to Dawn brightly.

"That's true. You'll need to be full of energy for the show," Terry said.

"I'm alright, one time I did four shows on the same day. You get used to days without proper sleep, grub or rest, so long as you make up for it after."

"Four shows? That sounds exhausting. Did you go out last night with the others?" asked Terry.

She looked at him, startled. "Nah, I don't like to drink. I just meditated and ordered food to my room. How about you?"

"Same here, I had a lovely Coq au Vin and French bread from a place down the road. Did you order from this restaurant? I wondered how the food was here."

She rolled her eyes at his tactlessness but indulged him anyway. "No, I ordered from Hatche, it's a salad bar not too far from here."

"Ahh great, great," he said, rocking back on his heels.

Dawn grinned at Jane. "By the way, I'm removing my name from the designs you're wearing in the show."

"What? Why?" Jane and Terry both appeared stunned.

Dawn faced Jane. "Well, I've been thinking, these competing are all up-and-comers, I don't need it as badly as they do."

Jane said, "That's so sweet of you, Dawn." She placed a

hand on Dawn's elbow.

"That is very gracious of you, Dawn. What made you come to this conclusion?" asked Terry.

"What do you mean?"

"But you knew they were up-and-comers from the start, didn't you? Why now?"

"Why are you battling me on this?"

"Honestly? I'm not sure you're telling the truth. Samuel Colton Jr promoting your brand would be massive for your company and you know it."

"Leave it," Dawn responded through gritted teeth.

"I will when you tell the truth."

"It's none of your business, Terry."

"It is if you're doing our group an injustice. You know we can't win if you change the branding."

She gulped and rubbed a hand over the back of her neck, staring at him with pleading eyes.

Jane turned to her. "He's got a point, Dawn."

"This is about more than winning."

"Is it? Because I thought we'd entered a competition," Terry snapped.

"Terry, this is Jane's final night, her curtain call. Let's keep tonight about that."

"Don't change things for me!" Jane spluttered.

"It's not just that. We're making a statement here, remember? And I won't lose out on this. If I call the brand 'Unnamed' and have the designer unknown, I guarantee people will want to want to find out who owns it. People love exclusivity."

Terry squinted one eye as though deep in thought. "Okay, so you will name it 'Unnamed'. For publicity?"

"Well, the idea was to keep the focus on Jane. But it could also work in the brand's favour."

"And in doing so, your brand becomes a mystery of its own. You might just get away with it. Okay, I'm in," said Terry.

"Me too," said Jane.

"But you know Colton won't sign an unnamed brand, don't you?"

"I won't need his signing if we make this work."

"Okay," he said, looking doubtful.

They didn't say another word about it as they stood watching the cars arrive in quiet contemplation, both happily oblivious, both thinking she was a marketing genius instead of a woman besotted.

# Twelve

On arriving in Las Vegas, they spent over five hours doing fittings, then with the make-up crew, trying hairstyles and make-up designs. Dawn, Angie and Jane spent some time with the photographers, working on poses for the pictures. Terry was taking pictures of everything at every stage. Dawn had gone into her usual organisational zone, but this time she had a weird jittery feeling in the pit of her stomach. She'd done hundreds of these shows and hadn't had nerves this bad in the last fifteen years. The shoes to one of her outfits were missing.

"Angie, could you go into town and find my black and white hook and loop shoes, please?" she asked. "We have thirty-four mins." She was staring at her watch.

Angie stared back at her, wide-eyed. "I don't think I can find those in thirty-four minutes, Dawn. Your store isn't even in the US. There's a mall nearby, The Simon Centre, I think. As far as I know, they have Gucci and Fendi. I could try to find something similar."

Dawn squeezed her cheeks together with her

forefingers. “I can’t put her in another brand of shoes with my special dress, Angie.”

“But it’s not your brand anyway, it’s unnamed.”

“I know that. It doesn’t matter. The shoes are part of the outfit, I will know they aren’t my design, and it won’t feel right.”

Angie huffed. “I know, I know, I just don’t see another way.”

“Wait!” came a voice. They both turned to see Delvin approaching. “I’ve got a pair of your black chunky heeled loafers in my box. What about them?”

“They’ll have the white strap missing, but at least they will be my design.”

“If it helps, I have some spare white strappy shoes I was trying out. I could change the straps for you,” said Gloria.

“Oh wow, you guys are the best,” she gushed.

Delvin ran off to find the shoes; Gloria went to fetch the straps. Terry stood beside her, his hand on his chin. His eyebrows raised. Dawn turned and looked at him.

“What?”

“Of all the runways, in all of the cities, I’ve never seen designers work together so well.”

Dawn smiled proudly. “I have.”

“And I suspect that’s because your kindness is the common denominator, Lewis.”

She swiped a tear from her eye, then turned back around.

“Angie, could you get Jane to make up, then check that our music and settings are as they should be?”

“I’m on it,” Angie said, walking away.

Dawn inhaled deeply before heading to the salon

to have her own hair and make-up taken care of, before changing into a black suit with a red jacket. A relief washed over her. Everything was coming together.

She pulled on a pair of silver and black Manolo Blahnik's, She wanted to look professional for the moment she'd be called onto the stage.

Gloria walked into the room and handed her the shoes. She stared at them, then looked up.

"Gloria, they're great, thank you so much."

"It's the least I can do."

Delvin ran in jumping up and down. "Samuel Colton Jr and P. Diddy are in the building," he said excitedly.

Dawn raised her eyebrows at him. "Breath, Delvin."

He inhaled dramatically. She held his hands and looked him in the eye.

"Are you ready?" she asked.

He stood and pulled his breath in, running his finger down his core meditatively. "I'm ready, Dawn Lewis, are you?"

"I am," she said with a smirk.

"I just saw your Jane by the way. She looks phenomenal."

Dawn's stomach whirled out of control; Delvin grinned at her. He hooked his arm in hers and Gloria's.

"Let's go do this."

***

During the show, Dawn was constantly looking out for Jane nervously. On the first clothing change, she went in and handed Jane the playsuit.

Terry snapped a photo.

“Looking good. Are you nervous about the dress? It’s a little brassier than your usual style, isn’t it?”

“It is. The shame is, it’s not going out branded as D-Lay, so I won’t get to see how the audience reacts.”

“Pity.”

She inhaled deeply and looked at Jane proudly. “You look beautiful.”

“It’s your vision, Dawny.”

Dawn turned to Terry. “It feels like one of my babies is going on stage for the first time,” she said, tears filling her eyes.

Terry wrapped his arm around her. “Ahhh, Lewis, are you crying?”

“I have an eyelash.” She laughed, and he looked down at her softly.

She went into the designer’s balcony for the finale. Delvin stood next to her, with little Lucy by his side. He pointed out his design, a sweeping grey dress that was beaded and tight on the top and ruched from the waist down. She was impressed and told him so. Then Miryam’s dress appeared, and she was pleased to see that Miryam had gone with her curtain style idea on the skirt, and it had paid off. It looked fantastic and got a lot of positive attention. The designers were so supportive of each other’s work and the atmosphere was electrifying because of it. She felt heat rush over her whole body as Jane walked onto the stage dressed in her design.

She looked spectacular in the feathered dress and cross over top, showing off her strong shoulders and long shimmering muscular legs. She heard gasps from the crowd. But Dawn found it strange to see Jane’s face so still and straight, like an empty vessel. It didn't look like the Jane she'd got to know, the Jane who had smoked a sneaky cigarette, blowing the smoke through thick, pink, smiling lips, who made fun of her getting hit on in a bar as they'd drank cocktails. Or who laid on her bed giggling, her hair splayed out beneath her. The Jane she'd met was like someone else entirely and watching the woman on stage she felt a mixture of excitement, honour, and something else. Something that felt a lot like arousal. Her breath hitched at the realisation.

She watched Terry as he held Jane's hand, offering support off stage. She couldn't help but feel jealous that he was with her, and she was not. She watched as he ran around at different angles taking photos, thinking how real Jane looked up there in front of everyone.

***

Jane slipped into character, gliding over the stage of a Vegas nightclub full of celebrities, journalists, and clothes designers. This was not new to her, but bearing her toned shoulders and legs, wearing something hand stitched by a woman she had become so fond of, was new, and it felt exhilarating. People recognised her and they were wowed – she could see it in their faces, in their gasps. She felt a thrill that she hadn't felt in so long. Terry held her hand supporting her onto the stage. He was always there offering his support and as she stepped up, she felt Dawn's eyes on her. She felt the silk gliding over her, felt a buzz running from her toes to her chest and back down again. And as the camera's flashed, she spotted Tom Woodley behind one, Terry Mack behind another, and she realised that she'd forgotten about the hole deep inside. She realised there was only one person watching who she was really putting on a show for.

She knew then what she hadn't realised before, something she'd known all along.

***

At the end of the night, Dawn watched over the balcony as the crew members packed away the contents of the stage and hall. She zipped up the dress and ran a hand down it. Terry came over.

"Are you okay?" He asked her with genuine concern.

"I'm good, thanks, Terry. I'm just watching it all collapse."

She stood quietly for several moments then turned to him. She'd always found peace in the clatter of the clean-up crew. She heard Terry inhale deeply.

"Are you sad that we didn't win?"

"Not at all. You?"

"No," he breathed. There was something in his tone, something regretful.

"Miryam deserved it," she said.

"Something tells me you had something to do with that."

"I don't know why you would think that, Terry," she replied, turning to smile at him.

"You're going to miss her, aren't you?"

"I didn't even know her that well."

"You know I don't mean Miryam."

She looked around at him. "She's just a model, Terry.

A colleague." But even as she said the words, she didn't believe them.

"Except you and I both know that isn't true." His tone was soft and unapologetic.

She didn't speak, but something in his words echoed through her. She would never see either Jane or Terry again, something that had never bothered her about colleagues in the past.

"I'll miss you, too." She whispered it so quietly that he wondered if she'd even said it at all.

"I'm going to transcribe my voice notes now," he said softly, turning away.

"Terry," she said.

He stopped and looked at her hopefully.

"Thank you for today. I've been nervous about the changes, and you've been there every step of the way."

He stepped closer, his hand went to lift, then he dropped it limply by his side. "I think you're remarkable, and that husband of yours should have treated you better. I would have been there supporting your career every step of the way, not making you feel like you somehow owed me for it," he said.

"But…"

"Stop making excuses for him, for one minute, would you?" He pulled a card from his pocket and handed it to her. She turned it over in her hands. "I know that you probably won't, but I'd love if you'd stay in touch. Or, at least, reach out to me if you need anything. Even if it's just a friend you need."

"That's so sweet, thank you," she said with a friendly pat on the shoulder.

He took a deep inhalation, stood still for a moment, then side-eyed her with a grin, before he backed away, still watching her curiously.

"If you need me for anything, anything at all, call me, okay?"

"Okay." She nodded, tucking his card into her purse.

She leant against the stage, thinking about what he'd said, wondering if she could love someone like him. His presence felt so safe. She turned her face to the side, still deep in thought. With a jump, she realised Jane was standing by her side. Jane's eyes found hers. Jane was a whole other story. Jane made her stomach lurch, made her crave something she didn't know.

"Where did you appear from?" she gasped.

"I've been here a few minutes. What were you watching so intensely, anyway?" she asked. They turned to face each other.

"Just enjoying the calm of the room."

Jane took Dawn's hands into her own and grinned. "Those designs were flipping amazing. It felt like I was at my peak, just like old times. Oh, my god, and when Shakira got up and did that 'shake your tail feather' thing with me. The journalists were going crazy. Did you see?"

Jane nodded. "It was amazing. You were amazing. What a way to make an exit," she said, hugging her. "I was so proud to see my designs on you."

"Thank you, it was an honour." She grinned.

"You're still glowing now."

"I know. I feel…" She exhaled heavily. "Happy. I'm so glad I listened to you in the end."

They smiled at each other, and Dawn had to remind

herself to breathe.

Jane said, "I'm going for a swim now. Wanna join me?"

"A swim? Weren't you invited to some crazy after parties with some crazy celebrities?"

Jane chuckled. "That's not my scene, and I'm not twenty anymore. You know that."

"Not your scene? What happened to all that talk about reliving your twenties?"

"If you remember correctly, it wasn't that I wanted to relive."

Dawn's stomach somersaulted as she remembered Jane's words.

"Look, after a hectic show, I like nothing more than to go for a swim. No paps, no gossip, just me hitting the H2O."

"You are very peculiar, Miss George."

"So I've been told. So, are you coming or not?"

Dawn exhaled and grinned. "Go on, why not? Give me a minute, okay?"

"By the way, I got P.Diddy to sign one of his hats. You know, for your son, Troy?"

Dawn looked at her, aghast. "You remembered?"

"Of course, I did."

"That's so thoughtful," she said, genuinely touched.

"Wait, I don't have a costume."

"So what? It's a private swim, babe. We can go in our underwear, or naked for all I care."

"Pah. Don't let Terry or creepy Charlie see us then – we'll be all over the front pages by tomorrow." She laughed.

***

They swam a few lengths of the pool, then Dawn sat on the side and watched as Jane swam back and forth. They both sank into the hot tub after.

"You're right, swimming is actually really refreshing to a tired body," she said, tipping her head back onto the side, the bubbles soothing her aching body.

"Told you. I always book the pool after a big show."

"Well, I can't see anyone else going in at 3am, anyway."

"I know, but just in case. I was hoping to get some peace before we have to fly back and go home."

Dawn looked at her and rubbed her chest. "Jane, if this is your quiet time, I can leave you alone? I'm ready to get showered, anyway."

"No, wait." She held her breath. "I meant peace with you, Dawn, not from you. Something came to me earlier."

She leant over and held Dawn's hand in her own under the water. Dawn looked at her, feeling a twisting in her core.

"I've really enjoyed spending time with you this week." She sighed. "Is it just me or is there… something between us?"

Dawn gulped. "I feel it too," she whispered. "But…"

Jane moved closer; their knees touched under the water. Dawn realised that she was about to kiss her, and she really wanted to kiss her too, but this was a woman. A model, in fact, who was married to a man. She could just see the newspaper articles now. What would her kids say? And Jane's husband? She moved away with a quick jolt. For a split second, she saw a look of horror on Jane's face.

Then her cool confidence was back. Jane turned around and walked up the steps of the hot tub, grabbing her towel.

"I'm gonna take a shower," she called.

"Jane?" Dawn called after her softly, tears of frustration blurring her vision.

"It's fine. Just leave it, alright," she said, walking from the room.

Dawn pressed her cheek on the cool tiles, her stomach was on fire. She thought about going after Jane and taking her into her arms. But she knew she couldn't go around kissing married female models. Not whilst she had kids sat at home waiting for her to return. The newspapers would destroy them both. She could see the devastation it would cause her loved ones. As she watched Jane walk from the room, it felt like she was letting a massive piece of herself slip away.

***

Jane stood under the hot water wondering if she had read the situation all wrong. She berated herself as she scrubbed her hair into a mass of bubbles. How could she have been such an idiot? She'd been so happy this week, happier than she'd been in such a long time, and now she had blown it in one simple move. She felt like such a fool. She couldn't explain what it was, but her whole body was screaming for her to not screw this up. She couldn't afford to lose this woman.

She played the moments repeatedly in her head. Them flirting on the bed, eating dinner in the café in Paris, the way they'd laughed together over the coffee and the dress incident, and how in the club over cocktails she'd felt like it was just the two of them in the room, everyone else was just noise and blurry lights spinning around their bubble. She was wondering what Dawn was thinking and feeling, and the frustration grew inside her belly.

She got out of the shower, dried herself off and pulled on clean underwear. Then she pulled at her phone.

James: *How did it go?*

Jane: *Great. But James, we need to talk.*

Immediately, her phone rang. She took in a deep breath and answered.

"I knew this was coming," he said. "You've weakened, Jane. All that talk of babies and pets."

"I don't think that's called weakening, James. Some might call it evolving or even settling down."

"I don't want to settle. Your priorities have changed. I knew things would have to end sooner or later. I just assumed it would be me who would come to that conclusion."

She tugged on her trousers, her temperature rising every time he spoke.

She bit her tongue. "Either way, you're right about one thing; our priorities are different now."

"Clearly. What happened to you? You used to be so driven."

"I'm still me," she said, holding the phone under her chin as she buttoned her trousers up.

"I used to be so proud to have you on my arm. Whilst the other men at the firm were nagged by their wives, my ambitious, gorgeous wife was doing her own thing, allowing me to do what I had to do to make it as a partner. And now look, I'm so close I can smell it."

She picked up her t-shirt.

"Wonderful."

"Oh, you're above that now, are you? Everyone admired us, you know." He went on. "You knew exactly what you wanted, and you went for it. If you retire now, I won't be home for dinner every night. You'll want to know where I am, why I'm not home. You'll get frustrated by my absence."

She let out a loud sigh. "So, this isn't about what I want, or who I am, but more about you wanting to be married and single all at the same time?"

"Well, freedom is a massive bonus in our relationship, yes."

"Can you hear yourself? Do you honestly think a marriage is about freedom, James?"

"From what I see, no. It's a bloody life sentence. But not with you, Gismo. With you, it's two people being who they want to be whilst enjoying holidays as a married couple."

"Holidays? Bloody holidays?" she said, watching Dawn walk through the changing rooms, fully dressed.

"Yeah, you blend with my family, you make the holidays feel special. And when we go away, you look like a goddess in a bikini."

"You know, James, I never realised how damn shallow you really are," she snapped, following Dawn with her eyes.

"Call it what you like, but you wanted it. You chose me and this life."

"I did, didn't I?"

"You did."

"God, what was I thinking?" she asked James, as Dawn walked out of the changing rooms and away.

She sat on the bench and put her head in her hands.

"Oh, come on. You know what you were thinking. I'm attractive, driven, financially stable. I take care of my body and I'm great in bed. Admit it."

"Who are you?" she spat. Suddenly, the room was spinning. "Oh, my god. I thought I knew you. I thought I loved you."

"You're saying you don't love me now? I don't see the others proposing, Gizmo."

"What others?"

"Oh, don't try and act all innocent now. Obviously, you've had other men whilst working away."

"Of course I haven't; I married you. My god, who do you think I am?"

"Fine, fine, I'll divorce you if that's what you really want. But let's get together first, talk about it. You know you're important to me."

"Wait, have you been seeing other women?"

"I wouldn't call it seeing, exactly."

"Then what would you call it, James?"

He winced.

"Oh, my god, what have I been doing with my life?" she screeched, more to herself than anyone else.

"Look, Gizmo, I've got to go. I'm flying home in the morning. Let's both sleep on this, both think about what we're giving up here, and discuss it in person. Okay?"

"Fine. But don't expect me to change my mind. As far as I'm concerned, this is over."

***

On the flight home, Jane and Dawn were both quiet and subdued. Terry tried chatting and making jokes, but eventually he lost interest and went away to mingle with the others. They drank prosecco, and when the afternoon tea came out they ate in silence. Every now and again her knee touched Jane's, and she wondered if Jane felt it or if she imagined the electricity.

Two hours in, Dawn fell asleep. Some turbulence soon woke her, and she realised Jane was also asleep, their heads resting together, their bodies facing each other.

"Think you need to put your belt on, Jane," she whispered.

"Huh?"

"There's a bit of turbulence," she breathed.

"Oh." For a moment she looked confused, and she lifted herself upright. Then she looked around and settled back into her seat, pulling on her seatbelt. "Okay, thanks," she murmured above her cable knitted blanket.

They laid in silence; Dawn saw Jane's eyes flicker up.

"You okay?" she asked.

Jane turned to her. "I don't know," she said, sadness in her eyes. "Is this it for us?"

The plane shook and rattled, and Dawn automatically reached out for Jane's hand. Under the blanket that was draped between them, they held each other's hands in silence as they rode out the bumps and drops of the clouds, her words bouncing around them, the veins in her wrists zinging.

Jane gulped. "What is it about you that has me feeling this way?" she murmured.

"Jane, I was married to Michael for twenty years. I was attracted to Terry when I first met him. But I've never felt like this, never had this need inside of me yearning to escape."

Jane held the tips of her fingers with her own, her eyes widening. "Me neither. What is that?"

"It's not just attraction. It's something else. I need you to know that I didn't pull away from you in the pool because I'm not attracted to you. I pulled away because it's so strong that it scares the shit out of me," she whispered.

"I get it. I'm scared too. But don't we owe it to ourselves to do something about it? Even when we first met, I liked being annoyed by you more than I've ever liked being adored by anybody else."

"I don't know. You're married. I have kids. We should probably just walk away and get on with our lives as though we never met," Dawn whispered.

Jane laughed sarcastically. "Can you do that?" she asked.

"With time, maybe," she said, biting her bottom lip.

"Then you don't feel the way I do," Jane said, turning away.

Dawn felt something biting at her. Could she really walk away from this?

# Thirteen

"We will shortly be descending into Heathrow Airport. Please could our passengers return to your seats and prepare for landing."

Dawn felt the final moments passing her by. She rolled onto her side and looked at Jane.

"Jane? I just think we have a lot to lose, getting involved. You're married, for goodness' sake. I mean, how would your husband feel?"

She watched the heavy rise and fall of Jane's chest. Then Jane turned to face her. She cupped Dawn's face in her hands.

"I know," she whispered. "You're right, you are. But…" She tailed off.

"But what?"

Their eyes met. "I've asked myself over and over, am I clinging to this woman because I'm losing sight of myself? Or even because my marriage is ending and I need to feel, something. But that's not what this is, I just met you at an inopportune moment. The truth is; I wasn't me, before you."

A tear spilt down Dawn's cheek. "I didn't know you felt the same way." She sucked in a breath. "I've been trying so hard to hold myself back, because I was sure about the way I felt for you. But I thought you were confused."

"I don't want us to go back to our previous lives. Not like this, it's bloody mad."

"Me neither, but what choice do we have?"

"Look, I'm stopping at the Windfalls tonight. Will you come with me? Please, Dawn, I just want to talk before we drive home."

Dawn gulped. She didn't want to reject her again, and the kids would be in bed by the time she landed anyway, and besides, she really wasn't ready to walk away just yet.

"Okay, just a chat. Then I need to get home. Okay?"

"Alright." She wiped her eyes. "I'm going loo before we land." She got up and walked towards the toilet. Dawn looked over at Terry, who was sitting on the other side of the plane typing away on his laptop. She rose and went over. She crouched next to him and looked at him, her lips pouted.

"Hey, friend," she said.

He smiled softly, leant down, and planted a kiss on top of her head.

"Never really had a chance, did I?" he said, pointing his eyes toward the toilet knowingly.

"Oh Terry, I've really enjoyed spending time with you."

"Yeah, yeah," he said, looking amused. "You take care of yourself, Lewis. Make sure she doesn't break your heart. And if she does, you've got my number, I'll come and sort her out."

She laughed at that, then stood up and walked back to her seat.

***

The Windfalls Hotel was a fifteen-minute drive from Heathrow. It had a private kitchen, balcony, an indoor heated private pool and jacuzzi. They sat in a large dining room, with an oversized glass of red wine each, neither of them speaking for a while.

Jane broke the silence. "Look, Dawn, I'm sorry if I came on too strong. I understand if you don't feel the same way."

"Jane, it's nothing to do with my feelings, and everything to do with your husband. You're forgetting that my kids and I all had to witness my husband's string of affairs through the media. Photos and stories came out to the public. Sometimes, before we even knew anything. That was a lot to deal with. I'm risking everything just being here with you. What I felt when I saw those papers." She sighed. "Well, I couldn't put someone else through that."

"God, I never even thought of that, did I? I'm so sorry, babe. But James and I, we've been over for a while. I've told him that when I get home, we need to talk. I'm going to end it, with or without you."

"So, why did you book this hotel instead of going straight home?"

"I needed to clear my head." Jane stared at Dawn. "I feel like I'm losing you and I've only just found you. And it's tearing me apart." She ran her finger around the rim of her glass. "How can I break up with him, whilst I'm so broken over you?"

Jane so badly wanted to touch Dawn. To show her

what she felt and yet, she couldn't, not until she ended things with James properly, not now she knew where she was coming from. Or she'd risk losing Dawn altogether.

She took a gulp of wine, contemplating it. "I've never cheated on James. I need you to know that. If I'm honest, I've never even known why people fight for love. It's just never been a priority for me. But it's as though I have no power over this connection with you. I am no longer in charge. Something else is at play." Dawn was staring out of the window and Jane wondered if she'd said too much. She felt a sense of dread wash over her. She put one hand on the side of Dawn's hip.

"Oh, Dawn, I…"

Dawn turned and met her gaze; she pressed her lips together. And Jane knew in that moment that she was falling for this woman. They stared at one another. Dawn's fingers moved slowly over Jane's skin. She felt as though her fingers were magnets, making her nerves stand on end with every touch. She inhaled deeply, intoxicated.

Dawn seemed to gain some clarity. She removed her hand and cleared her throat.

She stepped away and held on to the counter as though trying to balance herself. "I'm getting more wine. Would you like some?" she asked, picking up their glasses.

Dawn nodded, the normality of the gesture winding her. Jane pressed her hip against the counter and squeezed her eyes shut, breathing in and out.

Dawn stared out of the window, scared to turn back.

Jane wondered if she was losing her mind. She was a forty-year-old married woman. Men had thrown themselves at her all her life. And now, here she was acting like a needy teenager towards this woman who was blowing hot and cold constantly.

When she turned back, Dawn was standing on the other side of the room, scanning the books on the shelf. She picked up an old classic and read the cover. Jane placed down the glasses of wine. She ran her eyes over Dawn, noticing the hug of her jeans and the way her socks hung off the end of her toes. And she knew, in that moment, that she was in love.

Surely, nothing else could make a person celebrate such tiny details in another.

"Dawn." Her voice cracked.

Dawn turned away from the book in her hand and looked at her over her shoulder. Jane walked towards her slowly, as though not to startle her. Jane reached out and they linked their fingers together, neither of them speaking.

Slowly, their hands held on tighter, their bodies getting closer. Jane could feel the warmth radiating from Dawn's body, and as she moved closer, could feel her breath on her face. She held her own breath.

Dawn looked at her. "Why won't you look at me?"

Jane closed her eyes and sucked in a breath. "Because I'm afraid of what I might do." She whispered back.

A noise escaped her lips, and before she knew it her hands were on Jane's behind, lifting her up. Jane leant down and opened her mouth against Dawn's, welcoming her tongue as it plunged into her mouth. Dawn gasped, and they crashed into the bookshelf, sending books toppling to the floor. Jane's hands were searching Dawn's body, she so badly wanted to feel her skin beneath her tongue. She ran her hands deep in Dawn's hair, squeezing the roots as the kiss became deeper, more urgent. They pulled back and ripped off each other's t-shirts, and as their bare stomachs crashed together, they both gasped. She no longer cared what the risks were, or how wrong it was, it was just one moment in private, between two consulting adults.

She had never felt this raw desire to open herself up to someone, to have them open to her, to taste them. Dawn's hands slid down her stomach and stopped on the button of her jeans. Jane grabbed her hand and pulled it away. Dawn stopped and looked at her, breathless and feral. Jane took her hand in her own, and led her to the bedroom.

# Fourteen

Troy and Mitch stared open-mouthed.

"I don't understand. You were in love with her?"

"I was completely in love with her," she said dizzying, from the memory.

She wouldn't tell her son what happened after that, but the story still unravelled in her own mind. Their bodies sweating, tongues travelling over one another's skin. Jane's swollen lips nibbling and kissing all over her body. Their naked bodies rolling together, fitting together so perfectly, and their screams as they were slipping and sliding, orgasming against each other in a loud, fiery explosion. Both grinning, both gasping for air.

That part of the story really was only for Dawn's memories.

She took a gulp of wine, attempting to hide her quickening breath.

"You were compatible then?" Laughed Mitch.

"Mitch," exclaimed Troy.

"I'm sorry but damn, she slept with a famous bloody model."

“Pah.” He grabbed the empty wine bottle and shook it. “We’ve drunk it all. I’ll make coffee.”

“Sit with your mum. I’ll do it.”

They both stood and faffed about with a coffee grinder. Dawn stared out of the window, reminiscing. She remembered how they’d spent all night and most of the next day in bed, entwined in each other’s bodies, stopping only to drink water and get into deep conversations about the future and the past. She remembered feeling like every touch against her skin had been like ecstasy. She remembered realising what all the fuss was about. This was the reason people killed, died, and fought for love. This was why people made love over and over again. Because she realised what a drug sex was when the passion of lust was there. When you felt it like she’d felt it that day, sex needed a whole new name.

After making love, Dawn would run her fingers over Jane’s body, watching how she squirmed and laughed. She’d kiss her shoulders and neck and things wouldn’t take long to reheat. Jane had kissed Dawn’s tummy, skin damaged by pregnancy. She’d told her how beautiful and natural it was, and she’d told her she wished they could make babies together.

“There are options,” Dawn said, and Jane’s face had lit up.

***

Troy placed a mug of coffee in front of his mum, and she wrapped her hands around it, looking back at the boys as they sat with their own drinks.Dawn crossed her legs and laughed into the palm of her hand, embarrassed by the revelation.

"Mum, let's skip by the naughty bits and move on, shall we?"

"Of course, yes, let's move on."

# Fifteen

They woke the next morning, a tangle of naked limbs, white sheets, and hair splayed out. Dawn stretched and looked over at Jane. Jane looked back at her.

"Hungry?" she asked.

They ordered room service and sat in their pants and t-shirts eating omelette, fruit and pastries in the conservatory.

Despite the cold mist that lay across the garden outside, an autumnal sun shone through the glass, making it feel like summer inside. They basked in the warmth as they drank their tea and ate their croissants.

"Move in with me." Dawn said, so suddenly she'd surprised herself.

"What?"

"Move in with me."

"Are you serious?"

"Dead serious. I spent ages getting to know Michael before we would commit and look where that got me!"

Jane put down her croissant and pursed her lips. "But Dawn, there's something I need to tell you before you agree to this."

"I already know you're married."

"Not that." She smiled.

Dawn's eyes crinkled at the sides.

"Sometimes, I leave my thongs on the floor."

"What?" She let out an incredulous laugh.

"Let me finish. I don't know how to cook, like, I'm not being modest, I don't know how to cook at all. I don't know what I'm going to do with my future. I have savings, but I won't have a regular income. I get up super early, around 4am, to do yoga or go jogging. In the evenings, I like to laze around on the sofa and watch movies and eat popcorn or smelly peanut butter and celery."

"Jane." She laughed. "Take a breath! I kind of like the idea of picking up your dirty washing. I jog early, too, not 4am but fairly early. I love the smell of peanut butter and I really don't care what you do for a living. You aren't a bum. And you and I have something other people don't."

"What's that?" she asked, curling a leg up onto the chair.

"Advantageous serendipity."

"Advantageous serendipity," she repeated, throwing back her head in laughter.

"It's ironic, really. The men I've turned down because they might leave the toilet lid up or leave dirty socks on the floor. None of that bothers me with you."

"I'm sure it will after a few months."

"Then we will deal with it."

Jane grinned. "What are yours?"

"Mine? Okay, erm, well, as you know I'm a mum, so my kids will always come before anyone. I tidy up after them, make them food when they're hungry and generally give them a lot of attention because of the hours I work. I hate crumbs on work surfaces, stains in toilets and slowness. I don't sleep great, sometimes I wake in the middle of the night and go to my studio. I drink too much coffee and not enough water and I love fish, even though it stinks the house out."

After talking over the future, the past and all that goes in between, they went for a swim. Then took a long hot shower together. They used all the tiny, expensive body wash, washing each other's bodies from head to toe before washing each other's hair into a thick lather of bubbles.

Jane dried and straightened her hair and they both dressed and put on a little make-up, feeling almost human again. They took a walk around the local area, both prolonging the inevitable departure. Dawn called her kids to let them know there had been a delay and that she would be home by 2pm. Then she packed her things away and put her bag into the boot of the Lexus.

As they kissed goodbye in the hallway, things got heated and they ended up back in the bedroom. They made love once more. This time it was slower and more tender, as though they were both savouring the way it felt, as if they both knew sensed this would be the last time.

"I could spend eternity in bed with you, and I would never get bored."

Dawn leant up on her elbows. "Me too. And we have plenty of time for that. Right now, I really have to go." She reluctantly slipped on her jeans and t-shirt. She brushed her teeth and hair.

Jane pulled on a bed shirt with shorts and followed her from the room.

They stood back in the hallway and Dawn picked up her keys. When she turned back to Jane, she sucked in a breath, tears filling her eyes.

Jane raised her eyebrows.

"Stop. You will make me cry, too," she said, leaning over and wiping at Dawn's eyes with her fingers. "Why are we getting so upset?" She laughed, stamping her foot on the wooden floor. "I'm only going home for three days at most, then I will be with you again, in Leicestershire."

"I know, I know that too. And yet, leaving you here now feels so final. I'm so scared."

"Of what?"

"That you won't come back. That you'll change your mind, that he will somehow stop you. You said yourself that he can be pretty persuasive, Jane." Her lip wobbled as she said the words she feared the most.

"Oh, no chance. I'm besotted with you. He can say or do anything, but he won't keep me from spending the rest of my life with you." Jane lifted her chin and looked into her eyes. "Trust me. You're it for me now," she whispered, planting tiny, delicate kisses along her eyelids, her nose, then finally her lips.

Dawn wanted to melt in a puddle in her arms. She exhaled loudly. And Jane laughed into her tear-stained cheek.

"Oh, please don't make that noise. It gives me crazy flashbacks."

Dawn laughed with her. Her stomach felt like she was on a rollercoaster that wouldn't stop.

"Dawn, I need you to know something before you go."

She twisted her fingers together in front of her.

Dawn looked at her. "What?" she croaked.

Her eyebrows creased, and she breathed heavily. "I don't think I even knew what love was until I met you. It's like I have been sleepwalking through life with only my career in a type of tunnel vision. I think even if I'd have met you at thirty years old, I'd have retired right then. Modelling isn't what I was made for. You are."

Dawn felt her body collapse from the core, and she bent over. "Oh, my god, you're killing me. Do you want me to just come with you to collect your things?"

Jane leant forwards. She cupped a hand around Dawn's chin tenderly. "No. You need to see your kids. You know you miss them, silly. Go spend a couple of days with them, forget about me and I will be there before you know it, driving you crazy with my dirty thongs on your bedroom floor."

Dawn let out a groan and Jane laughed.

"I'm going to hold you to that. I'll be waiting, Jane."

"I'm coming for you," she whispered.

"That's so bloody hot!" she groaned.

Dawn kissed her hand with a deep inhalation, smelling the honeysuckle moisturiser on her skin, then finally, she moved away and walked to her car. It was drizzling with rain. Jane stood savouring the feeling of the drips on her hot skin. Dawn pulled down the cuff of her shirt from her wrists to dab under her eyes, as the rain got faster and harder. She closed the door and started the car engine. They stared at one another sadly through the swishing window wipers. Jane smiled and blew her a kiss as she reversed away, then she turned without looking back before the tears came down hard.

Jane stood on the crazy paving for several more minutes, widening her toes to feel the ground beneath her feet. The sky had darkened, and she knew that she too ought to head off. But maybe one more night wouldn't hurt.

Dawn's windows misted and she turned on the blowers, still watching Jane through the wing mirror as she stood outside, the raining pelting down on her. She was soaking wet and smiling and she couldn't believe she'd finally found what she'd been missing all along. She'd just never known it would be a woman.

# Sixteen

Dawn placed down her empty coffee mug and stretched out; she could feel a migraine coming on. She didn't say anything. These days she felt compelled not to mention any ailments. To her, it signalled the start of the decline. She'd seen that in her own parents and in her in-laws, too. First, they'd be complaining about this ache and then that. Next, they were giving you lists of people they knew who'd died every time you saw them, depressing the hell out of you. She couldn't allow herself to get that way. She rubbed her temples.

"Could I get a glass of water, please?" she asked.

Mitch stood up to fetch her a glass, this time nudging Troy back into his seat.

She looked around at the beautiful home her son had made for himself, so pleased that she had met Mitch and that he was such a nice person. Her son loved a good man, she could see that now – and that was what was most important to her. She also thought the fact that Mitch too was so involved in the fashion world had to be connected to the world Troy had grown up in. She knew that deep down everyone wanted acceptance, and she was there opening her heart to her son, offering a piece of herself in exchange for a small piece of his adult life.

Mitch brought over a tall glass of cold water, and she took it, her hands shaking. She sipped it slowly, hoping the pain in her head would at least abate until she was home alone. She knew that was when the sadness would come from bringing the past up, but she would overcome it – as she had all of those years ago. Now that she was older, she hadn't ever wanted anyone else. She found joy in watching her kids' growing families, baking with her grandkids, and watching the seeds of her vegetable garden grow in her greenhouse.

She did most of her own decorating and general household maintenance. She was content. She had experienced pure love, something she had never known even existed before the age of forty-three, and as much as it had hurt when Jane never came back, she had been glad to have had the memories, and to have experienced something so real. Jane George loved her, if only for a short time.

Dawn reached down for her handbag. Inside, she had the letter and a collection of magazine and newspaper articles. Her son was looking at her now, as though she were someone else, someone he was just seeing for the first time. And she held his hand.

"It's okay, son, you never need to hide who you are from me," she said, and a tear trickled down his cheek. She remembered the way he used to rub out his tears as a small boy, with his fists balled so tight. He would grind his eyes so hard she'd thought they'd rub out.

"You were so in love with this woman."

Dawn smiled at him and nodded.

"No wonder you looked in pain at Dad's wedding. It wasn't him getting married, it was because you never got your happily ever after, even though he was the one who cheated."

"I didn't begrudge him that. I was happy for your father, Troy. I watched them all day; the way they looked at each other, the way they responded to each other. It was as though they had their own secret language. And at the end of the evening, your dad even told me that, despite everything he'd done, he was grateful for what we'd had because he loves you kids so much. I had told him I could see that he was in love for real this time, that he was a different man with Lesley. And when he'd tried to deny it, I said, 'it's okay, I know about it too. And I'm happy for you.' Because I knew what genuine love felt like. I'd experienced it too, even if it was brief."

Troy put a hand over his mouth. "Mum," he gasped. "What did Dad say to that? Did he know you'd met someone?"

"I'm not sure. His eyes had widened in surprise, so I winked at him. He looked like he was about to respond, but he didn't. He just hugged me and said he loved me."

"That's so sweet," said Mitch, with his hand on his chest.

"You've really surprised me, Mum. I've always thought splitting with Dad had been the moment that your life changed. And tonight, when you first mentioned that you never loved Dad the way you should love a partner, I felt a bit pissed off, to be frank. But hearing your complete story,

I can see how it happened for you both. You were in an age where being gay wasn't 'okay'. Is that why Jane didn't come back? Were you worried you wouldn't be accepted as a gay couple?"

"No, that's not it. Of course, I knew it wouldn't be easy in the nineties, but I was naïve and in love, and I didn't see myself as gay. I believe you fall in love with a person. And it just so happened the person I fell for was a woman."

"That's such a bi thing to say, Mum."

She smiled. "Well, what about you, honey? Did you always know that you were gay?"

Troy turned and looked at Mitch, who nodded reassuringly.

"Yeah, I always knew," he said with a smile. "I have never been attracted to women."

She leant forwards and held his hand between hers.

"Then you know yourself well."

"Does Jamie know about any of this, Mum?"

"No."

"Will you tell her?"

"I don't think there's any need."

"So, why did you feel the need to tell me?"

"Oh, I think you know why. My boy, you needed to know that whatever it is you're feeling, I am here for you. I have been through it, maybe not in the same way, but to some extent."

"Yeah, I get it. I appreciate that, Mum," he said, hugging her. He leant back in his chair.

"So, how come you've never told me about this before? And why to this day have I never met this woman that's so important to you that you are visibly shaking?"

Dawn looked down at her shaking hands and sat on them. "I wanted to tell you, I did. I went to a couple of times, but words escaped me. And as you've already guessed, she never came back. Then I thought, why change things at home, if she's never coming back?"

"So, she's the reason you were so sad for a long time, and the reason you never wanted to meet anyone else? And also, I assume, she is she the reason you still went to fashion week every year without fail, even after you had retired. Am I right?"

"Partly, yes." She nodded and looked around thoughtfully.

"Fashion week was because you hoped to see her again?"

She smiled at him softly. "No, I already saw her everywhere. In every stranger's face that passed me by, in taxis, over busy roads, in supermarkets." She sighed.

"But why did she not move like she said she would? Did she reunite with her husband after all?"

"That's what I thought at first. I waited for a long time, glancing out of the window at every car, jumping at every ring of the phone. She didn't answer when I tried to call her. I left messages, sent texts, then I decided that she must have changed her mind. For weeks, I waited. I didn't sleep, I couldn't eat. All I could do was stare out of that damn window, praying that she still loved me. That this time it would be her engine I could hear, her finger pressing the doorbell."

A tear rolled down her cheek, and she noticed that Mitch, too, had tears of his own. He was squeezing Troy's hand tightly by his side, as though bracing him.

"I hadn't been out of the house the whole time in case she turned up. But I knew that I needed to quit. She didn't want me – I mean, for god's sake, she could have had anyone she wanted. I did think about going to find her… but fate made that choice for me. We had a nationwide problem with a material we used in our factory. I was called in for emergency meetings; I picked myself up and went in. I delved in deep, work seemed to plaster my pain. Then Jamie had a dance show, you had to have a back tooth taken out, and life came back to me. And one evening, as I was stitching a bespoke design for a very important client, my mobile rang. I got a shock when I saw her name on my screen. *Jane calling.* It had been over eight weeks. I was so mad, and yet, hopeful at the same time. But I couldn't answer it in fear of what she might say. It couldn't be good after eight weeks, I knew that. I let it ring off the first few times. But it just kept ringing. It was days before I answered.

But the voice on the other end wasn't hers. It was male. James introduced himself to me."

"Jane's husband?"

"That's right, he asked me to meet him, said he knew I'd been having an affair with his wife. I asked, 'is Jane okay?' He said, 'of course she isn't', asked, 'are you stupid?' I thought, surely, she wasn't that bad or why hadn't she come to me – I said I didn't know, told him I hadn't seen her, that she'd broken off all contact with me since being home. He growled down the phone, said maybe we should meet, to talk about things. I asked, 'why? If she doesn't want to be with me?' He snapped, 'Friday, 1pm, Caffè Nero on South Bridge.'"

# Seventeen

Dawn got a train to St Pancras, then a tube on the Northern line. She wasn't used to the tubes. There were people everywhere, rushing. She stood still, getting in the way and feeling lost. There were so many different directions and different coloured lines. It was busy and hot and every face that passed her was in a rush and unfriendly. She couldn't see which line went where. She found the whole experience nervy and a little irritating. She wished she'd just called for a taxi.

When she'd finally figured it out from a large map on the wall, her tube was due to leave. She raced down the escalators; it was getting hotter, the smell of burning rubber getting stronger the lower underground the escalators went. Her bag hit into the people she passed by. She apologised profusely but got no reaction. *They're like robots*, she thought. She jumped onto a full tube as the doors shut, but she got too close, and the doors reopened, holding up the train. She could see the passengers' eyes roll without even looking anyone in the face. There weren't any seats, of course, so she stood where she'd landed, by the door, staring into the armpit of a six-foot hairy man who had apparently also sweated to make the tube in time, or maybe he was just a sweaty kind of guy. She turned her head and glanced out of the glass door, looking through the reflection of everyone inside. She pulled at the collar of her jumper, coat and scarf around her neck, feeling sweaty and sticky, she needed to strip off, to stop her clothes from choking her.

As she stood gripping the pole, still warm from other sweaty hands, her shoes pressed into the rubber floor of the tube, body rocking to the bumps of the track, it suddenly dawned on her… what if James was a violent man? What if he wanted revenge on the woman his wife was leaving him for? What if he had Jane chained in the basement and had come to warn her off?

Scenarios ran through her head as the train jolted along. She got off at London Bridge with a lot of other people. Once out of the station, she stood to the side and checked the map, South Bridge it was almost a mile away. She glanced at her watch. It was 12.55pm, she would be a few minutes late. She hurried ahead, her coat flapping in the wind, the wind and rain assaulting her face, blurring her eyes. She came to a crossing, but the cars weren't stopping, she raced over between two cars, dropping her phone. She got out of the oncoming traffic, then headed back for her wet phone. When she arrived at the café, she was windswept, haggard and seven minutes late. And James was not there. She assumed that he had already left.

She meandered outside, slipped her phone from her pocket with her cold fingers and called Jane's number.

The man answered. "I'm outside," he murmured.

It was then that she wondered if she should have called the police first. "Why do you have her phone?" she asked cautiously.

"I'm outside," he repeated, cutting off with a huff.

Dawn wasn't sure what she'd expected, but she was met by a man in his forties. His hair was overgrown and unkept, his skin looked grey and haggard, his teeth looked yellow, and his shoulders looked as though permanently slouched. His clothes were hanging off him like they were two sizes too big, but he looked far from aggressive or capable of violence, he looked, she thought, emotionally battered. She wondered for a moment if he was ill. She perched on the wall beside him, still trying to work out what he could want to talk to her about. Was he there to say that he was dying, and Jane needed to look after him?

"Hi, James," she said, attempting to appear calm. "I'm Dawn."

"I know who you are," the man mumbled.

He glared at her; she imagined he might have been a good-looking man before this mysterious illness had taken a hold of him. He was tall with wavy hair, lots of facial stubble and piercing dark eyes. She tried to look beyond the self-neglect and self-loathing man in front of her, to a man who had once attracted Jane to him, enough for her to walk down the aisle promising the rest of her life to him. She tried to imagine them as a couple.

"We can talk in the pub," he said, and without any kind of acknowledgement he stood and trudged away as though expecting her to follow, and she did – begrudgingly. She followed him, along two roads and onto a quieter street, many times wondering if she should turn away and go home. Then she saw the pub on the corner and watched him disappear inside. She pushed inside, her eyes adjusted to the limited lighting, and she glanced around at three or four elderly men nursing pints of beer. The furniture and carpets, chairs and cushions were all decorated in dingy reds and browns; it smelt of stale ale. It was decorated how she remembered her grandma's house in the early seventies, where she used to sit at the wooden dining table and match her granny's sewing buttons from a giant glass bowl. This place, however, wasn't being ironic in their design. It had clearly been left this way since the seventies. He went to the bar, she sat at a large dark wooden table. A shiver ran through her. James brought back two whiskeys and a pint of lager. She stared at the glass in front of her.

"Oh, I don't day drink," she murmured.

"Just drink it."

"Excuse me?"

"Trust me, as you seem to be some kind of recluse hidden away from the media—"

"Excuse me?" she repeated, interrupting him. "I am not a recluse. I have also been pretty preoccupied lately. What is it? Divorce all over the papers or something?"

"I know you have, and I also know that my wife…" His eyes met hers. His lip wobbled, his voice softened. "She was in love with you, Dawn."

"Was?" She felt her stomach plummet as he pushed the letter across the table. Then he rubbed his hands over his face, pressing his fingertips into his eye sockets. She looked from him to the table and back. He gulped and pressed the palms of his hands together between his knees, watching her. She looked down at the crumbled paper, opened it out and read.

It was the letter to Dawn, telling her that Jane was about to leave James. She looked at him, searched his face for answers.

"What is this?" she asked.

"She'd written it for you. I found it in her coat pocket." He stalled. "She also came to me. Told me that she'd fallen in love. She said it was like nothing she'd felt before. That she was finally happy." He said the last word as though it tasted bitter on his tongue, and she could see his anguish.

They sat for a moment in silence then he looked at her, his jaw ticked.

"Listen, Dawn, I regret the way I reacted. I wasn't actually against this thing between you and her. Something had been missing between us for a long time. I know now that I should have been kinder to her, but my ego couldn't handle it and I reacted. I flew off the handle, I threw things, we screamed and shouted at each other. I wish I hadn't said the things I said. I wasn't even angry, not really," he said, screwing up his face, clenching his fists that were laid on the table in front of him. "I was happy that she had found someone to make her happy but... but..." His bottom lip quivered again. "But I wanted to feel that way about her, I wanted her to feel that way about me. She was genuinely happy. I could see it in her whole demeanour the moment she came home. It was the sparkle in her eyes, the glow of her skin, the bounce in her step. I had never made her feel that way. Never."

Dawn felt the sympathy for this man draining from her and being replaced with something more toxic as she put two and two together.

"James?" There was concern, clear in her voice. "What did you do to her?" she asked quietly.

His eyes widened; his forehead creased. He looked at her, then down at his lap.

"She told me that she was leaving me to be with… well, you, I suppose… she told me that she was moving out. Straight away."

"What did you do?" she repeated through gritted teeth.

"I tried to stop her from taking her things, and she stormed out. Said she would buy new clothes, said she didn't care."

"What d—"

"Stop saying that," he growled, leaning in closer, gripping the edge of the table.

A man on the next table glanced over, sneering as he swayed, a knowing look on his face. James's sudden contempt startled her.

"I didn't do anything. She got into her car…I told her not to go. She was crying and upset, and she got into the car. I told her…" He bent over and shifted his shoulders, then he slammed a wad of magazine articles onto the table making her jump from the thoughts spinning through her mind. But when Dawn looked down at the articles, she cried out in the middle of the pub, collapsing into a heap.

# Eighteen

Mitch's face paled. "Oh. god. Oh, Dawn.""What? What happened?" Troy was turning from Mitch to Dawn with a look of puzzlement. Which part hadn't he understood?

She pulled out the wad of papers that had been cut from the newspaper and magazine front pages, and she placed them on the table in front of them. Troy flipped the pages, reading each headline and taking in the photos. Mitch sat back and stared at the ceiling, and she realised then that he already knew of Jane's fate.

***Marrietta C George in mourning***
***Marrietta George exclusive interview on the loss of her beauty queen daughter***
***Death of a beauty queen***
***Jane George dead***
***Catwalk sensation driven to death***

One after another, all with pictures of Jane, on a catwalk, walking out of a mall, laughing in a pool, the club in Vegas and then… one of the cars, it's front half under the back of a lorry, the smashed window screens, a figure inside hunched over the steering wheel. On another was a picture of Marietta sobbing, her head against James.

Troy stared at the articles his head lowered.

"Oh, mum." He gasped, placing his hands on top of hers.

"So, you met Marietta at the funeral?" asked Mitch.

"I'd already missed it. I never got to go. There was a memorial on the anniversary of her death. I attended, but not for long, it wasn't my place to be there."

Troy looked at her intensely, eyes just like his fathers. "It's all coming back to me now. You'd come home from Paris so happy that year. You were baking and laughing and everything. Then life changed suddenly: you stopped going to work, was always in bed. Even Dad noticed. I was at his house one night. Him and Lesley were on a break at this stage, and he'd started dating someone new, I think her name was Melissa or Larrisa or something. I heard them whispering angrily, so I stood at the door, and I listened.

"There were pots crashing. 'Why can't we go to Rome Michael?' A voice whined.

"'I have the kids to think of.'

"'Can't they go to their mother for one bloody week?'

"'Nope.'

"'That woman is always working. She's their mother, for goodness' sake.'

"'She isn't working.'

"There was a rustling of fabric or something. 'So, where is she?'

"'Home, but…' he stuttered. 'I'm actually a little worried about her', he mumbled. 'I think she's depressed or maybe it's the menopause or something… I dunno, but she isn't herself. She seems so sad.'

"'She's not your problem.'

"'Of course, she is.'

"'Oh my… Urh… will she always come first, Michael?'

"'Not first. But she's my kids' mum, I will always love her. She's important to me, I thought you understood that.'"'I do, I just didn't realise there would be three of us in this relationship.'

"'You knew I had kids, if you can't handle it, you know what to do.'

"That was the moment I picked to go in and claim I'd been having a nightmare." He laughed. "I don't think I saw Melissa after that. I was so angry with Dad as well, for the way things had turned out."

"It wasn't his fault."

"You used to say that, but he was moving on with other women after cheating and you were so sad."

"He always loved Lesley; I think he just needed to be single to understand that."

"I don't suppose adult problems make sense to a teenager struggling with his own sexuality. I was so angry with him for ruining our family when I needed him, it's not been the same since. I wish we could have a better relationship with him."

"Troy, I'm positive you father would like nothing more. He loves you so much."

He turned to Mitch, who was chewing at his fingernails.

"Hang on, did you already know that she'd died?" he asked.

"It dawned on me earlier. But it wasn't my place to say anything, Troy."

"No, I know that. I'm not blaming you."

Mitch turned to Dawn. "I'm so sorry for your loss, Dawn."

"Thank you." She smiled. "It's been a long time now, though. She feels more like a dream to me these days."

"I can't imagine losing the person you love like that," he said, glancing at Troy, then bashfully turning away. "I actually read a beautiful article about Jane George in a magazine following her death."

"Oh?"

"It was a real testament to her. Some mag did a middle page spread all about her character. They had the best photos of her happiest moments, photos no-one else had, the journo must have been a friend or someone fairly close. They captured her so beautifully. Actually…." He paused. Gulped. Then stared at Dawn as though he'd seen a ghost.

"What?"

"Nothing."

"It's not nothing, what is it?"

Mitch looked down at his shoes, moving his feet side-to-side, then he looked up, a coy expression on his face.

"There was a woman in the photos with her. I thought for a moment then, she could have been you. But it wasn't, was it?"

"I doubt it, our time together was brief." Had it been another woman? A woman she didn't know about. She didn't really know much about Jane's life before her, aside from what had been in the media.

"I'll just see if I can find it online for you," he said, grabbing his phone. She wasn't sure she wanted to see the woman she loved with another woman. She'd always thought she was the only one.

"Thank you," she replied calmly, watching him type into the search engine.

Troy turned to his mum. "How did you get through losing her?"

"I had no choice," she replied, gulping in air. Taking her by surprise, her son leant over and hugged her. Mitch rose and went to the side of the chair and wrapped his arms around them both.

# Nineteen

Mitch stood and put their glasses, cups, and plates into the dishwasher. Dawn glanced out through the floor to ceiling glass doors. The daylight was fading.

Troy said, "I can't believe you kept that inside for so long." He had a look of anguish on his face.

"Hmmm, almost as long as you kept your secret," she said. "How long have you and Mitch been together, Troy?" she asked, wiping her nose on a bit of scrunched up tissue. She pulled her skirt over her crossed legs.

"About two and a half years," he answered coyly.

"I thought just as much." She smirked. "And there have been other men?"

"Yes, Mum."

"You didn't feel you could talk to me?"

"It wasn't about you."

"I know that. I just always thought you could talk to me."

"I can. I just wasn't ready."

"Okay. And are you happy?" she whispered, leaning towards him.

He glanced over at Mitch, who was putting a fresh filter in the coffee machine.

"Very," he whispered.

"Then share him with the rest of your family. You know they would love him too." She sat up. "He's a keeper. I'm happy you found him."

"Me too. But how did this become about me? Your revelation is massive, Mum."

"But it's the past."

"Not for me, I just found out."

"You're right, I'm sorry," she said, straightening the cardboard collar of her brightly coloured blouse. They sat in silence for a few minutes, the sound of the percolator heating and spitting in the background. Mitch busying around, wiping surfaces, and tinkering with pots.

"Was Jane the only woman?" he asked.

"Yes, she was the first, and there's been nobody male or female since her, I couldn't…"

He nodded. She looked at him, her face softening.

"You'd have liked her, you know. She was so young for her age, beautiful and bouncy. Freakishly strong, too." She laughed.

He smiled back at her. "I wish I could have met her."Mitch walked over and placed down a tray of coffee.

"Only one more for me. I shan't sleep tonight otherwise." She laughed, leaning over her crossed legs to pick up the cup and saucer.

Mitch sat down. "I could have made decaf. Would you prefer decaf?"

"Oh no, this will be fine." She smiled back at him warmly. "Troy said you did a master's degree at the

University of Birmingham? Fashion design, wasn't it?"

He leant one arm on the back of his chair, his body twisted halfway towards Troy. "It was, yeah. Yeah, I always wanted to be a designer. As a kid, I used to sew together my mum's clothes." He laughed. "She'd go mad. But as I got older, I'd be sketching out the designs that I wanted to make. It was a no-brainer to go into design really."

"And did you do an internship somewhere interesting?"

"Funnily enough, during my degree I got into graphic arts quite heavily and when I graduated, instead of going into fashion like everyone thought I would, I ended up working for a car manufacturer doing their graphic design stuff."

"Well, it's often in those trials you find your calling, but how did you then get into journalism?"

"Because although I enjoyed what I was doing, I still craved fashion. So on the weekends I started an online magazine. It was just a hobby, really, but people were really responding to it, and I had this funny sense of responsibility to keep feeding their curiosity. Now I have a readership of 60,000 and it's still on the incline. It was getting so demanding doing both this and my job, so I handed my notice in to pursue it – and I've never regretted it for a minute. I love it."

"What a fantastic story, Mitch."

"Thank you."

"You're like a power couple, my boy, the high-flying solicitor and his boyfriend, future media tycoon."

He laughed. "Hardly a tycoon, it's an online mag."

"Well, you never know, one day. Everyone must start somewhere."

He nodded, and she pursed her lips.

"Actually, Mitch, maybe I can help you out a little."

"You can?"

"Why not? Yes, let's finally let the cat out of the bag on Unnamed."

"Seriously?"

"Seriously. Book me in, I'll give you the exclusive interview, the story of a brand unknown, and the women who revolutionised the modelling industry."

His eyes doubled in size. "Are you kidding? That would be a dream come true. I just thought it inappropriate to ask you for an interview, as Troy only just introduced us as boyfriends. But that would be fantastic."

She hadn't even flinched at his words. It was Troy whose breath seemed to hitch up a notch ever so slightly, almost so slight it was unnoticeable.

"Oh, it'll be fun," she marvelled, looking from Troy to Mitch and back. "Like a visit into the past…" She smiled brightly.

"I'm so happy, that would be just amazing. Thank you." He leant forwards in his chair.

"Thank you, too. Don't think I haven't noticed how well you're looking after my boy. We thought we'd lost him for a while. But he's happier and I feel like he's coming back. I think you might have had something to do with that."

"I don't think that's my doing, Dawn. Troy has been doing a lot of work on himself over the last twelve months. Haven't you, Troy?"

"Oh, you realise I'm still here then?" he said with a grin.

"Sorry, of course I know you're here."

"It's okay. Having him by my side has made me realise how much more I want to be."

"We help each other," he said, fanning himself with his hand.

"And that's what a real partnership is all about. And Mitch, I have to say this house is very well designed and also very clean. Not Troy's strong point, so it has to be you, or at least your influence."

Mitch laughed.

"Heyyyyy," Troy yelled.

"Well, she does have a point, Troy." He turned to her then. "He is very unorganised and scruffy, I think he thinks pots have feet of their own. On the other hand, though, his cooking is divine."

"Is it now?" she pondered, thinking back to her son's kitchen phase before he hit the pre-teens.

"Yep. Our friends literally invite themselves over for dinner at this point. They go crazy for his lamb chops in pesto with broad beans."

"Sounds amazing. He always did love cooking. He'd throw together some real combinations. He would leave pots and pans everywhere," she explained with a flair of the hands. "God, I used to get so cross. I'd come in from work to a kitchen full of mess, and my husband would send me on my way saying, 'it's okay, he's discovering himself.' It would drive me insane. I was a big believer in discipline and all I could see was mess, mess, mess. But Michael, well, Michael saw beyond the mess."

Troy looked at her. "Oh, Mother, don't start getting all soppy on me now."

"If it helps, I still don't see why you couldn't be creative and all that and still clean the dishes as you went along," she added pointedly.

Troy laughed. "Dad always ate my creations, too."

"He did." She nodded with a smile. "I could never bring myself to try one, I never knew what you'd put in them. I also spent way too much time with women with a BMI below eighteen."

He laughed. "I think you'd like my concoctions now."

"I think so too," she said with a nod and a smile.

"Well, that's settled then," marvelled Mitch. "You're coming over for dinner with us and our friends one evening. How about Saturday?"

"Hold on, Mitch, that's a busy night. Greg, Callum, Nish and Jackie might be a bit much for Mum. But you definitely should another day, Mum, I would love that."

"I would love to, thank you. I'm sure your friends would be fine, I'm not such a prude." She wrapped her long fingers around her chin. "Anyway, boys, I'm so glad that we finally had this chat. I couldn't be any prouder."

"We've enjoyed it, too. I'm so pleased to have finally gotten to meet you and know you, I'm not sure what Troy here has been so afraid of all of this time. Maybe one day he will introduce me to the rest of the family."

"Oh, Mitch, they will love you. Jamie is Troy's biggest ally, and his father Michael really is a wonderful man."

"Let's take one step at a time, shall we? Mum, it's been a great evening. Apparently, I only knew a fraction of who you are, but nevertheless it's been great getting to know all about Jane. Aside from the sex bits."

At that she laughed. "I thought I was very PC. A son

doesn't need to know every ounce of his mum's life."

"No, a son certainly doesn't." Troy laughed. "Although, I can't believe you spent over twenty years of your life in a marriage that wasn't right for you, then lost the love of your life in mere moments."

She placed her hands in her lap and sighed softly. "I'm just grateful to have finally met her, and to finally have fallen in love so spectacularly."

"But you never got the opportunity to know what that relationship would have been like in the real world. And you never met anyone else after. Doesn't that make you sad?"

"Not at all. I feel lucky. I had a good relationship with your father, three amazing kids and a career. Not many women can say that. My relationship with Jane was just…" She inhaled deeply. "Something else. It was the icing on the cake. What if we'd stayed together and the relationship had failed, or we'd discovered we didn't like each other all that much?"

"That's a funny way of looking at it."

"I just wouldn't want my time with Jane to be diluted. I'm afraid if I meet someone else, then she would disappear forever from my mind."

"That's crazy, Mum. She died, you lived. I'm sure she would have liked to have known that her death hadn't ruined your life."

"It hasn't ruined my life. Everything challenges us and changes our perspective. I'm still enjoying life. I have you guys, those beautiful grandkids of mine and… I have my very own beans and carrots growing in the garden."

"Can you hear yourself, woman? You have your beans and flipping carrots. You're Dawn Lewis. Don't you feel mad at the world for taking her away from you so quickly?"

"No!" she said with a snigger. "I was very fortunate to have even met Jane. Not everyone gets that opportunity to meet the one."

"And you chose to share it all with me, now. After all this time."

"Yes, because you've been choosing to keep a huge part of your life separate from your family. Troy, you think that life must be this linear thing. You think I'm so together. But we all have dilemmas. We all feel emotions beyond our control, and I want you to celebrate your uniqueness, not turn it into this shady thing that needs to be hidden away."

"I just wish you'd told me earlier."

"I could say the same for you, I mean, would it have really made any difference?"

"Some."

"How?"

He looked down at his feet. "I was young and still figuring things out, but your sadness, it made me feel somehow inadequate. Like I was letting you down."

Tears sprang to her eyes. "Oh, Troy, you could never have let me down. You kids are the best thing that ever happened to me. Parents don't always make the right choices, just what we think is best at the time. But sometimes I do wish I'd told you, and if I'd have known then that you thought my unhappiness was remotely anything to do with you, I absolutely would have told you."

"Me too, Mum," he said, wrapping his arms around her. She leant forwards and squeezed him tight, hiding her tears in the shoulder of his top.

# Twenty

Dawn made her way into Leicester. She was doing an interview with Mitch, then afterwards Troy was cooking the three of them dinner. She knocked on the door, there was no reply. She knocked again. Saw the curtain move. Heard banging.

"One minute," Mitch's voice came. He opened the door.

"Dawn. Hi." He sounded out of breath and surprised.

"Hi, Mitch, sorry. I'm a little early, aren't I?"

"Oh, it's fine."

He opened the door wider to let her in. A man was behind him putting his shoes on. Dawn walked through to the kitchen as Mitch saw the man out. She sniffed at the pungent aroma. Weed. She opened the kitchen window. Sniffed some more.

She sat down at the kitchen table. Smooth jazz music played in the background, creating a peaceful ambience.

"Troy not here?" she asked, as Troy walked back into the kitchen.

He combed his hair with his fingers and stretched, his

belly popped out over his trousers. Self-consciously he pulled his t-shirt down with both hands.

"No, I'm sorry, there's actually a good chance he won't make it back tonight. He was in the gym this morning when he was called in to court to cover a case that wasn't his. The only thing is… the case was in Kent."

"Ahh, I see, no dinner then. Does he stand you up a lot?"

"Oh, I don't see it like that, he's not standing me up. His job is demanding. He's making his mark in the world. And after all, I'm hardly fighting crime sitting here writing about fashion and celebrity gossip."

"It's talented, what you do. My only concern is that you're here all day alone. Doesn't that get lonely if Troy is working long hours?"

"Sometimes, but I have friends."

"Oh, yes, like the one that just left."

His body tightened at her tone. "Sort of," he said sceptically. "Still want to do the interview? I could order us take-away?"

She looked him over.

"Okay, I've not had Chinese food in a long time." she said, immediately having doubts; *Would this be awkward, just the two of them?*

Later in the evening, they were cross legged on the rug eating Chinese food from the foil tubs, delving back into the past. They spoke about all of the work that went into each fashion week, the models, the hotels in every city, and the celebrities she had met.

"What was it like being a mum and a designer for the stars?" he asked.

She put down her fork and took a sip of wine. "I was lucky enough to have a fantastic support network around me, which is important. My ex-husband was a great father. I also took my kids to fashion week on many occasions. My son never did get to meet P. Diddy, but he did get an autographed hat that my friend Jane George got for him. My daughter got to meet Miley Cyrus, who was one of her role models. She almost passed out when Miley took her on stage to sing a Hannah Montana tune." She laughed. "But I've been fortunate enough to have three fantastic humans for kids."

She spoke about the group experiment in Vegas for Marilyn Marshall.

"Am I right in saying you later exposed Marshall Media about the immoral way they treated the guests on their show?"

"I can't take the credit for that, we teamed with an amazing journalist. I can't mention his name for legal reasons. However, he helped us, and many other artists in that room who were set up by Marshall Media, by exposing the truth. His job was to follow us through the creative processes of the competition, and he also captured lots of conversations that they had manipulated with their own cameraman. You must remember, this was before YouTube or social media. So, at the end of it, he took all of the TV show clips and he put each one together with the real conversations and used them in the court case that went worldwide."

"That's amazing. For our listeners, Marshall Media shortly closed down due to the expense of the court case. Despite that, evidently, these shows created a growth in reality TV."

"A growth? Wasn't it the start of them?"

"Not at all. We've done reality shows in this country since the 1960s to seventies. But as far as I can remember, they never actually hit it big until the around the millennium."

"I never really watched TV, Mitch, so personally I'd never seen anything like it. I wish I had, maybe, then I would have known. It was pure exploitation, although, of course, nowadays reality TV is mostly acting. It wasn't back then."

"You say that, Dawn, but people still get set-up and exploited even today. I mean in comparison, I bet there's worse being aired today. And yet, it ultimately was the collapse of Marilyn Marshall's foundation, wasn't it? Despite most, if not all, of the contestants gaining from it."

Dawn narrowed her eyes at him. "Are you implying that we shouldn't have taken action against her?"

"God, no, I wasn't minimising what they did. Today, people are fully aware of what they're entering into. And they make the choice that the gain is bigger than the loss. They accept fame over their own mental well-being. But the show was rather experimental, and none of you really knew what you were walking into. You couldn't play the system or have a tactic. You didn't know that what you said would be manipulated, and you were under pressure. They were wrong not to make you aware of the consequences. My point was that some very famous designers were unknown before it, weren't they?"

"Oh, absolutely, my brand D-Lay was already doing well, however, my label Unnamed was born of that show. Also, Gloria Bailey, who you've obviously heard of as a massive international designer nowadays, was totally unknown when she went on the show. She was grabbed by Samuel Colton; he had his own design of her animal-free fur coat and blended it with her plant-based leather handbag at the music awards and got her designs noticed. The great thing is, she's a lovely person, very respectful of the trade and what it stands for."

"Really? I did not know that was her big break!"

"Absolutely. She was also a big part of the court case rallying in lots of support. Oh, and Delvin Summers! He was such an angel."

"I see, so despite the bitching and moaning on the show, you guys were somewhat bonding?"

"Oh, absolutely. I made some great friendships from the show. We really pulled together when things got tough."

"And you were teamed up too, right?"

"Yes, eight teams, of which included a model, a designer and a journalist."

"And who were your teammates?"

"Terry Mack from *The Look* magazine and model Jane George."

"And your team were set to win, weren't they?"

"Yes, although by removing D-Lay and changing my branding to Unknown, ultimately it took us out of the competition. Although, Miryam was a great designer and she deserved to win."

"Even to this day, you weren't named in the competition, although anyone who knows who you are will have seen you on the show. So, what on earth made you remove your brand like that?"

"I wanted the show to be about empowering beauty and style. So, not naming that brand was important to me. If that doesn't make sense, I'll simplify it. It's almost like colouring in the main parts of a picture and leaving everything else shaded in the background. I needed Jane to really stand out, to be able to educate others of the restraints around fashion."

"Restraints?"

"Remember, this was the nineties, Mitch, but it still exists today. We have learnt to accept and not question what's drip fed to us from birth. But people have this idea of who fashion is for, and it's stereotyping and exclusive. I really wanted to get into the crux of that. I mean, I think these days we are coming into an era of questioning our expectations, which is fantastic. But we mustn't penalise people who aren't aware. It's a really hard pill to swallow for some people because it's beliefs that are buried deep. However, I feel it's part of our jobs, in the spotlight, to recognise that not only those within the boundaries of a created version of perfection can enjoy or celebrate fashion. And if you ask me, the fact that even someone like Jane George was insecure about her looks, it really highlights the hypocrisy of it all."

"You're telling me that the beautiful model Jane George was insecure about her looks?"

"I am. She was absolutely stunning, and she had those famous broad shoulders and those amazing thick thighs from the amount of gymnastics she had done in the past, which was an achievement that should have been celebrated. But instead, she was regularly asked to cover up her shoulders and thighs and ridiculed for being 'masculine'. And this message that we, as a team, wanted to put out there, it really opened up some doors in the respect of designs for everyone. It got the ball rolling and, of course, nowadays woman are viewed much differently, we've come over the hypocrisy hump a little.""And it couldn't have come sooner. And speaking of which, Jane George really had this reputation for having no personality too, didn't she? People described her as almost statue-like. I'm led to believe you actually formed quite a bond with her in the short amount of time you spent together. What was she like in real life?"

Dawn paused and inhaled. "Now, I want to be careful what I say here, not to do her an injustice. Jane George was..." She paused, the images of Jane running through her mind. "She was spectacular. She was funny, she was smart, and all she wanted was to be a good role model. I mean, you think about it – for how beautiful and rich she was, she didn't even seem to notice. She was humble, and she made this decision that if she slipped with her emotions, starved herself, if she got drunk in the public eye, or only wore designer clothing, that she would be a bad influence on the young people out there looking up to her. She just took that responsibility to the maximum. Hence, her reputation as this plastic, unmoveable doll. She saw that reputation as a necessary sacrifice for her as a role model. It was great in so many ways, but it was also a shame, because she was hiding so much of herself, things that were just normal human emotions. And, in fact, she was a very kind-hearted woman. Her dream was to give it all up and buy a big house in the country and to foster lots of children."

"She wanted to be a mother? That's certainly a side of her you never saw in the public eye."

"No, not many did and, in fact, I only knew her for a couple of months, and it only took that – well, actually less for me – to love her."

"You loved her?"

Dawn looked down at the cuffs of her shirt, pulled at one, then looked at Mitch.

"I did. And people will make of that what they will. I can't control the media – that's the give in freedom of speech, I suppose. But I just want to put it out there that it isn't a crime to love someone. Love between consenting adults should be celebrated."

Dawn knew that those last words were the nail in the coffin the very moment she let them out. She had wanted to say she loved Jane without letting on that it had been a sexual relationship. After all, Jane had technically been married at the time, and whilst she had tried to rectify Jane's reputation of being plastic Jane, if Mitch shared that part with his readers then everything she had said would be forgotten, all but for one part. Jane would be classed a 'cheat'.

"Okay, I'm sorry, but the question on many readers' lips now will be, what does that mean?"

Her heart dropped into her stomach, and she stared at him. He was staring over her shoulder as he spoke.

"Were you and Jane George in an intimate relationship?" he asked.

She sucked in a breath, looked down at her shaking hands. "Pause," she snapped.

He looked at her.

"I said pause, Mitch."

He reached over and paused the Dictaphone; his fingers were shaking.

"What kind of journalist are you?" she snapped.

His eyes widened and his head moved back from the neck. "Dawn, I didn't mean to offend you. We can discuss what goes live after. I just wanted to give you the opportunity to explain this unique situation. I know what it's like trying to hide who you are. I honestly thought it might help you, to share your truth."

"By bashing the woman I loved when she's no longer alive to defend herself?"

"That's not what I was trying to do. Listen, you have the power here. I know your story; I know how you want Jane to be interpreted. Together, we can show this for what it is. Two women who, in an open society, may have never married the opposite sex in the first place, had they had the choice."

The doorbell rang and Mitch hopped up from his chair.

"And how do I know you won't go behind my back and write what you want for publicity?"

"Because your son wouldn't love someone who would do something so underhanded."

The doorbell rang again.

"Sorry, I won't be a moment. You probably need a break anyway." He walked out of the kitchen, placing a hand on her arm as he passed her.

"Is he actually using my son's integrity against me?" she murmured to herself.

She glared out at the garden, irritated. It was starting to

rain; she stared through it, her mind continuing to wonder through the sound of Mitch talking to another man in the background. As her breathing calmed, she saw images of Jane laying on the bed laughing, Jane standing barefoot in the rain outside of the London suite, blowing her a kiss, holding back her tears. Her lip trembled, and she took a deep breath.

She turned in her seat and tried to peer through the gap in the door. Mitch was talking to someone in the entrance in hushed tones. She could just see his muscular shoulders and wide smile.

Who were these men coming and going whilst Troy was out at work?

"This isn't a good time," she heard Mitch say. And he showed him out of the door, promising to call him back later.

When Mitch entered the kitchen, Dawn was up, bag in hand, ready to go.

"Dawn?"

"I'm going now." She knew she was being hasty, jumping to conclusions.

"I thought you wanted to see Troy?" he stuttered.

"Maybe another day," she called, tripping over herself to get out of the house before she said something she might regret.

***

As soon as Dawn got home, she called Jamie.

"I think Mitch is sleeping around behind Troy's back."

"Wait. Rewind. Who is Mitch?"

"Troy's boyfriend."

"Troy has a boyfriend?" she gasped.

"Oh, sorry, yes, I was supposed to have dinner with him today."

"Mum!" Jamie complained. "Why have you not told me this? If you have met him, this is massive."

Dawn told Jamie the entire story about meeting Mitch and him asking to interview her, about the men at the house, and her concerns.

"What was he interviewing you about?"

"That's another story for another day."

"But you told Troy?"

"Because I wanted him to open up to me."

"Like a trade of information type deal?"

Dawn sighed. "More like, trust for trust. Jamie, I had a fleeting relationship with someone who was famous in the nineties." She gulped. "And they were killed in a car accident."

"You had a what with a what?"

"It's not a massive deal, Jamie. I was in love briefly after your father."

"And he was killed?"

"They were killed in a car accident."

"Oh, my god, you poor thing! Are you okay? It must have been devastating talking about it, after all this time."

"I'm fine, but I'm worried about Troy. What if this Mitch guy is cheating on him?"

"I have to admit, it does sound sketchy as hell. Shall we drive to his house and spy on him?"

"Don't be ridiculous. I'm going to have to tell him, aren't I?"

"Maybe don't go in there saying he's cheating, maybe

ask who the people are… do you want me to come with you?"

"I'm not sure, because he doesn't even know that you know yet. And if he is cheating this could get really messy, so I'd rather deal with it alone at first."

"What do you mean messy?"

"Mitch knows things about me, that will make big news. In the grand scheme of things that isn't my concern, but I'd rather you not be witness to it as well."

"What things about your mystery man who died?"

"Woman."

"Woman?"

"It was a mystery woman."

"What?"

"And she was famous and married."

"What? A married woman! What were you thinking? You know how much we were hurt when Dad cheated on you! Ooooh, this is a lot, Mum."

"I know, I know. It wasn't an affair, exactly; they were on the verge of breaking up and she broke up with him. I think she was on the way to me when she was killed."

"Who was she, this celebrity? Would I know her?"

"Jane George."

The line was momentarily silent. "Was she a Gucci model in the eighties?"

"Yes."

"The one with the eyes?"

"The one with the eyes," she agreed.

"Wow. I didn't know she was lesbian. Come to think of it, I didn't know you were, either, so shows how much I know."

"I'm not. We were both married to men first, we just fell in love with each other, it wasn't intentional, it was just… bigger than the both of us."

"Then I'm sorry you lost her, Mum. I'm sorry you never got to be with her."

"Thank you," she whispered. "Listen, don't mention anything to your brother, please. Let's just get more info on this Mitch guy first, okay?"

"Of course."

"Now, how are those beautiful grandbabies of mine?"

Jamie laughed. "Currently, they're terrorising the neighbour's dog."

***

Dawn huddled into her coat. "We should have got a cup of coffee to walk with."

"There's a little shed thingy, about halfway around the park. The lunchtime rush will be about gone by now."

"Okay, we can go there, if you like?"

"Okay. But I don't have long, Mum, I've got another meeting at 2pm. What's going on?"

"I can't meet my son on his lunch break?"

"You can, but you never have before."

"I just wanted to check that everything's okay."

"Everything is fine. Why?"

"Well, I hear you're working long hours. Relationships take work and time, you know."

He looked at her coyly. "And you'd know about that?" he teased.

"Learn from my mistakes. That's why I know about that."

"Well, thank you for your concern, but Mitch and I are fine. Here, the coffee place is open. What do you want?"

"Just black, no sugar."

As he stood in the queue, she watched him, thinking how vulnerable he looked. She remembered the little boy he once was, with his curly hair and perky personality. All she wanted was to protect him from the hurt of the world. He approached slowly, handed her a cardboard cup, and they continued following the park path around.

"I imagine Mitch gets lonely, doesn't he? At home all day whilst you're always at work."

"Why are we still talking about this?"

"Okay, I'll drop it. And besides, he has all of those friends to keep him company, I suppose."

"That's right, we do have lots of friends."

"Yes, I know. Two of them came around when I was there the other day. One youngish man with red hair, and a large muscular man later. Good you've got lots of friends."

Troy stopped walking and turned to face her. "He's not Dad, Mum. I'm not worried about who he has over when I'm not there."

"No, no, I'm sure you aren't. It's good you've found someone you can trust."

"I do trust him. So, stop worrying."

"So, you know who they are? The redhead and the muscular man?"

"Nope, and I don't care. So, drop it."

"Fine."

"Also, Mitch wants you to go round and approve the article. He thinks you hate him because he quizzed you about your relationship and you immediately left. He won't post anything you aren't happy with, Mum."

She sipped her coffee. "He just caught me off guard, that's all. I'll pop back around tomorrow after swimming."

"Good. Don't dismiss him until you get to know him, he's a good bloke."

***

"I told him I'd pop back around tomorrow. Troy wants me to keep my nose out, so I'll have to."

"You shouldn't have given him a time; you should have turned up unexpectedly."

She chewed her nail. "I could just go now? That would be unexpected."

"Do it. Did Troy tell you he called me?"

"No."

"One sec, Mum." She yelled, "Mark! Can you get Jake off that wall, please, it's not safe." Dawn heard him muttering something in the background.

"Sorry about that, Jakey's got into this climbing stage. He's on everything lately. Anyway, he called me, because he reckons, he's popping around on Sunday, for me to meet someone. I said I'd make Sunday dinner. I take it you started that ball rolling."

"Well, that's one good thing, I suppose. Unless Mitch is cheating. God, he'd be so embarrassed, he'd never want to involve us again."

"Let's keep our fingers crossed then. Go now, call me when you get back, to let me know how it goes."

***

Mitch opened the door a quarter of the way open and wedged himself into the gap. Dawn felt her eyebrow rise.

"Dawn! How are you?" he asked loudly, glancing behind himself.

"Very well, thanks, Mitch. Troy said you wanted to discuss the article?"

Her attention was caught by a movement in the window. Her eyes met a pair of familiar eyes. Then, the man backed away from the window. She glanced back to Mitch, anger building in the pit of her stomach. She glanced back to the window. Mitch dropped his shoulders in defeat and swung open the door.

"C'mon in."

She peered at him as she walked into the house.

He asked, "Can I get you a tea? Coffee? Water? Whiskey?"

"No, I'm okay, thanks," she replied stiffly. "I've not long had a coffee."

He flicked on the kettle.

"I feel like we got off to a bad start yesterday and upsetting you is the last thing I want to do. But there's something else I need to tell you now, and I hope this won't further annoy you."

"Is it, by any chance, that there's a man hiding in your lounge?"

He rubbed his head and exhaled loudly.

"I was trying to hold this off, but I clearly need to introduce you. One minute."

He walked out of the room.

"What?" Was he going to introduce her to his other boyfriend? She rubbed the back of her neck.

She turned around and Mitch was standing in the kitchen doorway with the man. He was muscular but a fair bit older than Mitch. He was wearing a black t-shirt and dark denim jeans. He had a strong jawline, a rustic looking grey and black beard, and piercing grey eyes. The eyes looked so familiar, she could almost remember looking into them. She thought she remembered having a conversation with him, thought she remembered kindness and affection from those eyes.

She was convinced she had spoken to him before. But where?

"I don't understand. Mitch, who is this?"

# Twenty-one

Dawn took the coffee from Mitch; she hugged it close to her chest and looked across the table at Terry Mack. Editor-in-Chief of *The Look*, currently the second best-selling magazine in the UK. The man who she read had won awards for his charismatic storytelling and humanising abilities, the man who she'd read was on the top ten eligible bachelors list after his divorce several years ago.

The same man who, twenty years ago, had followed her around like a lost puppy. Who had stood at her hotel doorway with takeaway food, embarrassed to see that she had already made plans, who had watched her fall in love with Jane, and had whispered into her ear, 'I never had a chance did I?' A man who she had never spoken to since."Oh, Terry, I'm so sorry that I didn't recognise you."

"It's been a long time, Lewis," he said with a grin. "You, on the other hand, you haven't changed a bit."

She laughed. "You always were a smooth talker."

"Never worked on you though, did it?"

She looked up through her eyelashes and smiled at him coyly.

"Ahh, what did I expect? You were in love. It was so bloody plain to see."

She smiled at him. He nodded and smiled back.

"You were just a boy of twenty-four." She laughed, her face cupped in her hands, her elbows rested on the table.

"Well, I'm all man now." He grinned back at her with a cheeky sparkle in his eyes.

She laughed and a tear rolled down her cheek. He reached out and placed a hand on top of hers.

"But, honestly, I wish you'd kept in touch," he said softly. "I could have helped you through your loss."

"I didn't want to give you the wrong impression. You seemed vulnerable."

"Always such a lady." He smirked.

"You're too kind," she said with a grin.

He rolled his eyes.

"I've not seen your designs around much lately."

"No, I sold D-Lay not long after everything." She didn't mention that she carried on running Unnamed, that it had peaked too soon, and died almost as fast. Although she suspected he already knew that. She didn't want to get into it, it still hurt. She remembered the moment she finally admitted defeat, how worried she was, and that she finally understood the fear she'd seen in Jane's eyes when she'd suggested being herself for the final show. She wondered if they'd have been happier, retiring together.

"And Unnamed went under too?"

*So, he'd chosen to go there.* She felt her fists clench beneath the table.

"It did, eventually." She said, gritting her teeth and smiling, softly.

"That must have been hard. It was your passion."

"It was, when I was young, hopeful and driven." She blew air softly between her lips. "So, how do you know Mitch?" she asked.

"Funnily enough, he called the paper last week. Someone in my old office came and told me that a guy had called in wanting an article I had written twenty years ago and that he was willing to pay good money for it."

"So, you wrote the middle page spread he was raving on about."

"Apparently so." He grinned. "The call intrigued me. Then, when they told me he wanted it for you, I thought it couldn't possibly be you that hadn't read it. And so, I asked for the caller's details and I called him back myself. Low and behold, this guy tells me you never saw the damn article."

Mitch stood by the table, his hands and coffee gesticulating as he explained his venture, whilst sloshing coffee over the chairs and floor.

"Yeah, and then he asks me, 'this is for Dawn Lewis?' I told him, 'yes'. He snaps, 'why did she not read the damn article when I wrote it?' I was surprised for a moment. I hope you don't mind, Dawn, but I explained the circumstances to him and then he went deadly quiet. I was terrified, thought, I've said too much. Then he goes, 'I don't want your bloody money. I want to come with you to make sure Dawn Lewis reads the sodding thing, in front of me.' I was genuinely confused, like, why does the editor of *The Look* magazine want to see Troy's mum reading his twenty-year-old magazine article so bad?"

Dawn glanced over at Terry. He was watching her.

They grinned at each other, like two people who shared a secret.

Mitch, completely unaware of their shared moment, continued his account of their situation, like he was the star of the show. "So, I asked him quietly, 'do you know her personally?' He says, 'yeah you could say that.' So, I told him he could come, but I said I'd need to check with you first."

Terry leant back, one arm hanging over the back of the chair. Grinning, he joined in on the conversation. "So, I turned up, before he had a chance to talk to you," he said. "But when I got here, he asked me to leave because you were here, and he hadn't told you I was here yet. Then today, he was telling me how he couldn't tell you, because he'd somehow messed it all up. He'd upset you. Laughable nonsense, really, the way this guy handled the whole thing."

Dawn grinned, looking back and forth between them.

"So, you're not cheating?" Dawn laughed.

Mitch looked at her, his brow furrowed. "Cheating?" he exclaimed, spilling what she could only assume was the last of his coffee. "God, no. Troy is all the man I can handle."

"Okay, TMI. So, the red-haired guy who was here really was just a friend?" she asked, taking a sip of her coffee.

"Oh, no, he was just a wedding planner."

She looked at him wide-eyed. "You and Troy are engaged?"

"Not yet." He grinned. "I'm planning on proposing this week. So please keep it quiet. I was thinking now that most of his family have met me, I can finally take this to the next level. I'll explain it all to you, but for now, why don't I leave the two of you to talk?" He walked over to the kitchen sink.

She smiled and shook her head, then turned to Terry. "Alright, let's see this article that I should have read twenty years ago."

He reached down into his bag, and pulled out a laminated magazine, placing it onto the table in front of them. Terry slid it over the table to her. It was *The Look* dated the 1st of September 2001. She flicked through, coming to the middle pages, and she gasped, the images filling her with a pool of emotions.

"I knew it," Mitch gasped. "The woman in the pictures was you!" He was standing by them, his hand on his chest. She didn't respond, too shocked as her eyes worked across the double pages.

The headlines read; ***Jane George; the happiest days of her life, mere moments before her tragic death…***

Clear, brightly coloured photos of Jane, a look of pure happiness on her face. She was standing on the podium in the studio, the green dress half stitched. She was looking down at Dawn who was grinning right back up at her, whilst stitching the hem of the dress. Dawn had on faded blue jeans, a white crinkled shirt, her hair was in a messy bun, her glasses on the end of her nose – she'd forgotten what she looked like post-Jane. It felt like she was looking at someone. A couple, in love.

Dawn put her hand to her mouth. "We were putting together the outfits for the Vegas competition."

The second picture was Jane jumping out of the pool, a look of peace on her face, her hair wet, slicked back.

"She loved to swim after every show." Dawn sighed.

The third was a picture of the two of them, running over the cobbled roads of Paris, ducking from the rain. They looked so carefree.

She pointed at the page.

"That was right after I'd completed the outfits. We had just ten hours left in Paris. I remember it vividly because we hadn't slept at all. But we were determined that this time we were going to see Paris like a pair of tourists." She smiled and stroked the picture.

"I knew you were up to something. If you remember rightly, it was also the night I brought you dinner. You were dressed in that clingy black dress." He swooned and she felt herself blush. "You looked so beautiful. I thought another man was taking you out. And, feeling all depressed, I went for a walk in the rain. I looked up, and low and behold there the two of you were, running out of the hotel like a pair of skiving teenagers. You looked so happy; I just couldn't resist."

She smiled at him, then looked back down at the paper.

"You know what's funny? In that moment, I felt kind of relieved that you were sneaking out with her, and not another man. Little did I know at the time."

She turned to the fourth image; Jane peeping from behind the curtain of the stage, looking into the crowd. She followed her eyes, and there she was, in the crowd, admiration on her face. There were several other smaller Polaroids dancing around the page of the article. Some in Vegas, with the Bellagio behind them, some in front of casinos. Photos they hadn't even known were being taken, when they'd snuck out alone. They were private and natural. She would have been angry at his intrusion of their privacy, but he had captured the emotions of the moment so beautifully that all she wanted was to bathe in the photos, to be alone to cherish them.

She read Terry's description of who Jane really was from his time spent with her. No-one could have described the woman she had met and known and loved with so much respect and knowledge, no-one had shown her personality so perfectly.

His voice startled her. "You once asked me how I knew about you and Jane," he said softly. "This." He pointed to a picture.

She squinted. Jane was sitting on a small wooden boat. Dawn was climbing into it, holding her left hand. She had an ice cream cone in her right. They were looking into each other's eyes as though holding back laughter. She was bent as though pure joy was trying to burst from her insides out.

She remembered that they were laughing because they'd snuck off again. This time into a Vegas casino where they had gone on a rollercoaster before drinking frozen strawberry Daiquiris whilst walking through the fake streets of Paris, as though they were back there. Terry had found them climbing onto a boat in fake Italy, sharing an ice cream, and had snapped a photo. She stared at the pictures until they disappeared into a blur.

Terry placed a finger on her cheek, collecting tears she didn't know had spilt. She looked at him, her wrinkled finger stretched out across her chest. "You made it look so beautiful," she whispered.

He wrapped his arms around her, and she felt the

protection of his hard body. Everything about him took her back to the happiest time of her life. Except now, he seemed so much bigger, despite being the same size. He pressed his lips into her hair, the way he had the last time he'd seen her.

"I'm not a creator, Dawn. I just find what is already there."

# Twenty-two

Dawn pulled into the parking space at Pittsford waters, a place she hadn't visited since the kids were young. Terry was already standing behind his Land Rover with a border collie by his side. He gave her a little wave and came towards her as she got out.

The doors of her car clicked to lock as she walked away.

"Well, good morning."

"Good morning." She looked him up and down.

"This is Ralph," he said as the dog walked over to sniff her trainers.

"Hello, Ralph," she said, patting the dog.

"Don't think I've seen you in running gear before."

"You neither. Suits you though," he said, nudging her. "You ready to go?"

"As ready as I'll ever be," she said, beginning a slow jog. "If I go too slow, feel free to jog off ahead. At sixty-two years old, I know my own pace. Don't want to be aching tomorrow."

"And the same goes for you, of course," he remarked, smiling a lopsided smile.

Matching each other's easy pace, they turned the corner onto the lake's path. Ralph jogged along ahead of them happily.

"Mitch seems nice," he said.

"I don't know him too well, but I'm getting that impression too. I wasn't sure about him at first. Although, that was because he was keeping secrets about the wedding planner and about you, I assumed he was a dishonest person."

"He went to a lot of trouble to contact me, you know. To get those photos for you."

"I bet he did."

She picked up her pace a little, and Terry followed suit. She knew he still had plenty of fuel in the tank.

"He invited me over for dinner tomorrow."

"He told me. Are you going?"

"Will you be there?"

"I will."

"Then so will I."

"I think he wanted to thank you for coming with the articles. And maybe introduce you to my son, Troy."

"It'll be nice to meet him. If you don't object, of course?"

"Of course, I don't. You'll like Troy, he's a character and a half."

They jogged up a hill, and despite herself, Dawn gave herself an extra push.

"So, what have you been doing with yourself all these years?" she asked him, beginning to feel the strain.

"Less than you'd think. I moved from London to Kettering, where I bought a house."

She looked at him then. "A woman?"

"You could say that." He chuckled.

As they jogged, they joked and laughed easily. Talking about memories of Paris and the mistakes they'd made since. They stopped to walk at the 10km mark.

Terry breathed heavily, his hands on his knees. Dawn carried on walking. He caught up with her.

"Look at you! Not a hair out of place. I think all that talk of being sixty-two was to throw me off my game."

She nudged him and laughed. "You're kidding, I'm knackered."

"I'm an old man too, you know."

"Not as old as me, Terry."

"I'm not that far off, c'mon."

He'd walked her to the car and turned to face her. "This has been really nice." He said smiling. He leaned in to kiss her cheek.

"It really has." She smiled back. She knelt down. "Nice to meet you too, Ralph," she said in a baby voice. Terry grinned. Ralph jumped up and licked her face.

"Ralph, you big flirt," he joked. "He gets more action than me these days."

"I'm sure he does." She laughed, walking away. She felt contented and safe being around him. It was like she was suddenly younger, desirable again. He'd always had her on a pedestal, and she never knew why.

As she slid into her Audi, she looked back at him. He was standing at his car, the door open, watching her, a soft glint in his eyes. She closed the door and started the engine, butterflies swarming her stomach. She flicked on Radio 1 and when she glanced into the wing mirror, she realised she was still grinning. As she left Northampton, she sang along to Ed Sheeran, as she made her way back onto the A6. She slipped into the middle lane around an eighteen-wheeler lorry, remembering something she hadn't thought about in a long time: how she used to picture her perfect relationship.

She remembered the vision she used to have of them cuddled on the sofa watching bad TV, a fireplace blazing beside them, jogging by a lake laughing and joking, eating, drinking, and connecting, and she realised that someone had somehow slipped into the image of that blurred out figure in her mind. Now all she could see in its place was Terry Mack.

She laughed at herself for being an old fool and decided that after dinner the next night, she shouldn't see him for a while. She knew she was fantasising about being with him because of all of the old emotions of Jane that were being evoked. They had long ago been put to bed and she couldn't go making an idiot of herself now, at her age. She was a proud woman and she'd done just fine without a man for the last twenty years.

***

After a great night with Terry, Troy and Mitch, Dawn argued with herself a lot, but decided not seeing him would be for the best. She spent the next few weeks busying herself; she cleared out the old studio and did some painting. Painting led to drawing skirts and tops and suits. She took Mia and Jake out to the park, then on to Gallone's ice cream parlour, before visiting the horses by her house. She picked up a handful of magazines and went home, where the kids had fallen asleep in her bean bag chairs after such an eventful day. She made herself a cup of chamomile tea and flicked through the magazines from her bag.

Most of them were fashion magazines, but it hadn't been an accident that she'd picked up *The Look*. When she'd opened it, she had seen Terry's face in a small circle on the first page, beside some editor's notes about spring bringing with it new life, and she felt hopeful. Inside, he'd also written an article on Kate Middleton's public display of affection to her prince, and an article called *Twelve Ways a Dog Can Strengthen Your Relationship*. At that she'd laughed at the irony, remembering Terry and Ralph jogging by her side. She grabbed an apple from her fruit bowl and took a bite, glancing over at her beautiful grandkids sleeping peacefully. She sucked in a breath, feeling her lungs fill fully for the first time in so long.

# Twenty-three

Dawn sat at her kitchen table, her glasses hanging on her nose. She pushed a piece of the jigsaw into its gap. It was a photo of her grandkids splashing in puddles at the farm park. Her phone rang.

"Hey, Jamie. What a coincidence, I was just looking at Mia and Jake."

"Looking at Mia and Jake?"

"Yes, I was doing that jigsaw puzzle you bought for me last Christmas."

"Oh, cute. So why didn't you answer my facetime?"

"Facetime?"

"Yes."

She picked up her 'world's best grandma' mug and sipped her tea, spotting a missing wellington boot piece. "I don't think that thing works on my phone, Jay."

"It should. I'll take a look when I see you. But I called to see if you've checked your post yet this morning?"

She smacked her lips and put down her tea. "No, why?"

"Go and check."

"Okay, hang on."

She rose and made her way to the front door, pushing her glasses up the bridge of her nose. There was a pile of post sprawled over the matt.

"I have a couple of adverts for driveways and gutter cleaners, a bank letter and… hmmm, wait, there's a beige envelope handwritten in calligraphy. I assume this is the one you're getting excited about?"

"Open it. Open it," she cried.

Dawn opened the envelope, pulling out a card. She read it and grinned, the phone perched under her chin.

"They're getting married. In, oh my. It's in Paris," she said, releasing air from her lungs. "And I have a plus one." She laughed.

"The 26th of June. That's only four months away."

"Wow, they don't waste time."

"I know. I'm so happy for him. He's nice, isn't he?"

"Despite my initial hesitations about Mitch, yes, he seems nice."

"I also checked out his online magazine. He's actually very talented. I didn't see your article though. Did you approve it?"

She sat back down at the kitchen table, the post still gripped in her hand. "I approved it. It's very good. Very Travis Barker bare all kind of a deal."

"What are you on about? Travis Barker had a drug addiction and a sketchy past to overcome."

"I'm not comparing myself to him. But I was in love with a very iconic woman. Her mother was a household name. You just need to read the article. He's going to upload it on the 1st of September."

"That's ages away."

"I know, but it will also be the twenty-two-year anniversary of her death. It will represent a celebration of her life."

"What a sweet idea. Did he come up with that?"

"I think it was Terry actually."

"Who's Terry?"

"My friend."

"Oh, okay. Well, do you think Mitch would let me have a sneak peek of the article now?"

"I don't know, no harm in asking, I suppose."

"I'll ask him. Now we just have to find you someone to take as your plus one to the wedding."

"I'm happy to go alone."

"Oooh actually. Mark? Mark?" she yelled. "Is your lesbian aunty still single?"

"No, she's with that woman that works for Vodaphone, remember. Remember, cus you asked her if she could get you a discount."

"Oh yeah! Ah okay, never mind."

"I don't want setting up, Jamie. I'm happy as I am. I don't have time for dating, anyway," she said, sipping her tea.

"Says the retired woman. You should try working whilst caring for two kids. Oh, wait, you did, didn't you?"

Dawn laughed. "Sort of, and I know it can be difficult. Although I always found the internal battle the hardest, the 'am I psychologically damaging my kids by not being there?' thing."

"Ahh, that one, I've passed that, I have the unabridged version now," Jamie said with a half-yawn, half-snigger.

"You do? Lucky you," Dawn joked. "You sound tired. Go get a nice cuppa and put your feet up."

"I'll try. So, no set-ups then?"

"Nope, no set-ups, please."

"Okay, looks like I'm going to be too busy anyway. I'm certain they'll need my help getting it all organised." She sighed.

# Twenty-four

Dawn opened the door and Mitch shuffled in.

"It's like the Niagara Falls out there," he complained, pulling off his jacket and shaking it out.

"Come on, I've just put the kettle on."

She lit the fire, and they sat down hugging their mugs to them.

Mitch sat in the armchair. "Well, I don't know what you said, but Troy went to play golf with Matt and Michael yesterday."

"He did? Mitch that's wonderful news."

"I agree, from what I hear it went really well, too. He was even talking about us going over there for dinner soon."

Dawn smiled.

"It was Matt who suggested golf, as well. We went for a drink with him and Joanne on Thursday night. And Troy said he wants to reconnect with his father. Just came out and said it all blasé. Honestly, I was so happy, Dawn," he said, hands on chest. "You know his family means so much to him and it hurts him when he communicates all wrong."

"I know he doesn't mean it when he lashes out. I think he just spent so long not understanding his own emotions."

"Whatever it is, he's slowly coming round. I think the chats to you have helped."

"And the work he's doing on himself."

"And the work he's doing on himself, absolutely. I love him just the way he is, but Dawn, these tweaks he's making, they are like the fine tuning of him."

"I'm so pleased," she marvelled. "Where is he today?"

"He went to see a client in Chichester, so I thought I'd come and update you on the wedding deets," he said, placing his empty mug on the table.

"Alrighty, what can I do? Throw it on me."

"Oh, you don't need to do anything, I just wanted to tell you about our plans."

"Well, there has to be something?" She could hear the disappointment in her own voice.

"Just sit back and relax. It's all in hand," he said proudly.

"The seating, the food, the flowers?"

"Everything."

"Everything?"

He nodded. "I paid for a full package wedding. Our friends from Brighton are the best wedding planners. They let us choose everything down to the cutlery. And we got in at Chateau Lignon last minute. Thanks to your Terry."

"My Terry?" she exclaimed.

"Yes, he knows someone, who knows someone. They have a four-year waiting list minimum, and they found a spot for us as a favour to him. We were just so happy. He said he's been calling you, by the way."

"So, you're somehow friends with Terry now?"

"Yes. He's amazing. He said he's going to do the photos for us, too."

"So, he's coming? To the wedding? How did this happen?"

"After you left the other night, we just got talking. One thing led to another and…"

"And what?" Her voice sounding deeper and louder.

"And," he said calmly, "I told him about the wedding."

"Oh. I see," she said, straightening up.

He narrowed his eyes at her then. "Convinced I'm a cheater, aren't you?"

Her shoulders deflated. "Oh, Mitch, I'm sorry. It's not you. Well, it is you. But it's only because I need to get to know you a little more before I can trust you fully."

"Whatever happened to innocent until proven guilty?"

"I know, you're right. Can we try again? Please?"

He turned to her and held her hands in his. "Of course. And even if I was a cheater, that man is as straight as Queen Victoria's dresses."

She grinned at him, impressed.

"I'm not joking, Dawn. When you went to the bathroom at our house, the man could not take his dirty little eyes off your bum."

She laughed and gave him a playful smack. "Don't be dreadful." She placed a hand to her burning cheek. "So, I suppose I'm going to have to adjust to the fact that Terry is coming to the wedding," she said with a sigh.

"It wouldn't hurt to look spectacular either," Mitch said with a grin. "You know, show him what he's missing."

“I’m a designer and mother of ‘the Troy’, darling, of course I’m going to look spectacular. This is going to be so bloody awkward.”

He looked at her coyly.

“What? Oh god, what’s that look Mitch?”

He leant forwards, squeezing the bottom of his chin. “Hmm, probably shouldn’t have added the plus one to his invite then?”

“You gave Terry a plus one?”

“Ermmm.”

“This is a disaster. What if he brings a date? I’m not even taking a plus one.”

“He probably won’t either.”

“Probably? Probably isn’t good enough, Mitch. Pah, I wonder if Mark’s lesbian aunt is free that evening,” she muttered.

Mitch raised a concerned eyebrow at her. She put her hand on his arm. “I’m kidding. Either way, it’ll be fine.” She laughed, feeling the dread in the pit of her stomach.

He smiled. “You’ll love the location, Dawn. They have this pianist with a singer; they make the kind of music that makes you want to cry. And it’s so scenic, all of the green hills and a vineyard or two in the distance,” he said, swiping his hand over a fake skyline. “I’ll show you pictures – it’s slightly south of the centre of Paris, and it’s right in the middle of a field.”

“Sounds wonderful. How many have you got coming?”

“We wanted it to be small and intimate, so we only invited fifty-seven.”

“Have you had many responses?”

“Just people who called me excited, but it probably

covers about twenty-five. I don't suppose everyone will be able to travel at such late notice."

"No, even with home weddings it's normal to only get about eighty per cent turnout."

"It will be fine."

"You need help decorating?"

"No, the flower company are putting flowers and ribbons all over the garden. I've also ordered a flower wall for photos."

"You certainly are very organised, and creative too. Do they have guest rooms?"

"Yes, I'm reserving them as I get confirmation."

"Drinks?"

"They have a bar; I've also ordered champagne from a local winery."

She laughed then, standing to take their mugs into the kitchen. "I'm impressed with how organised you are, Mitch. Need help with the suits?"

Mitch walked in behind her. "We were just going to buy them off the rack."

She spun on her heel. "You will not. No, I won't have that. Let me make them!"

"That would be wonderful. You really don't mind? It's short notice."

"It is, but I can do it." She grinned.

"Also, why do you care if Terry brings a date?"

"I don't."

"Now try saying that without a million expressions written all over your face."

She pouted her lips at him. "You're very pushy for someone who's just about to join the family."

He grinned. “Stop deflecting. You like him.”

She didn’t respond, just looked out over the garden.

“Can’t say I blame you. The man is a god.”

Dawn’s hand flew to her mouth, then she snarled at him jokingly. “You don’t need to tell anyone about this conversation,” she said, walking away.

At this, Mitch threw back his head and laughed.

# Twenty-five

It was a sunny morning in June when the plane descended into Paris. The sky was a pale blue, highlighting the start of summer, and Dawn could see the Eiffel Tower in the distance. As they disembarked, her son Matt added her bags to his trolley and sat his son Lucas on top of the pile. The eight of them trundled through the airport. Dawn was quietly watching her family as they chatted and jostled excitedly along the narrow-carpeted tunnel of the airport.

She walked beside Matt. "What time are Michael and Lesley flying in?" she asked him.

"Oh, they flew in with Troy, Mitch, and the wedding planners yesterday. Dad and Troy wanted to try out the local eighteen holes."

"They played golf in Paris?"

"Apparently it's where they go to talk now."

"I'm so glad they're getting on."

"Me too." He grinned.

***

They reached La Campagne à Paris by 10am, their taxi van coming over the brow of a dusty hill upon a chateau that was nestled in a field amongst trees and bushes. There were several cars and vans dotted around, one delivering flowers, another champagne, and a catering company. They all trundled out of the vehicle and walked over the stoned drive to a set of enormous front doors. Instead of approaching the doors, they followed a woman carrying boxes of shoes around the back of the building. There, a large gazebo stood proud, inside was a band. They were setting up their equipment. Caterers were setting out tables with napkin swans, wine glasses and cutlery. A flower wall was being installed, and lots of white chairs lay across the lawn ready to be unfolded.

Dawn's eyes swept the activity and stopped on her son, Troy. She could see that he was laughing, engaged in a deep conversation with Terry. Her stomach lurched. Terry looked as gorgeous as ever in a white Ralph Lauren shirt and casual joggers. His beard was shaved, his hair waxed over into a side parting, and his hands rested on the shoulders of a young petite brunette with a button nose and shiny hair, who was dressed effortlessly in yoga trousers and a floaty vest. Dawn turned away and went to find somewhere to park her bags. She was shown to her room, up a set of crooked stairs with low ceilings. Jamie, her husband and kids were given the room next door. She unpacked her case and hung out her dress for the celebration, putting it in the room to air. She splashed water on her face and topped up her mascara before making her way down the stairs.

Dawn went into the garden and stood beside Mitch;

she was pulled into hugs. She caught sight of Terry and the pretty brunette being shown around by the wedding planner, who she recognised from Troy's house.

"Did you get the suits?" she asked, turning her attention back to Mitch.

"We did indeed! And they look remarkable. Oh, Dawn, that material," he gushed.

Dawn smiled brightly. She'd ordered the material from an old supplier in Peru, where she'd found it in a tree in the eighties. "I'm glad." She looked up to the sky and inhaled clean air. "You could not have picked a more perfect day for a wedding." She sighed happily.

"Have you spoken to Terry and Katie yet?" he asked.

"Not yet," she said with a gulp. And before she had the chance to ask any more questions, Mitch was swept away by caterers wanting to know where to place the hot plates.

***

As Troy and Mitch stood at the trellis in their smart suits, grinning at each other, Dawn couldn't have been prouder. The sun was setting behind them, and the stars were making an appearance in the clear night sky. The piano played quietly in the background as they made their promises and exchanged their rings. Terry stood by Dawn's side with his brunette to his right. She felt a tear roll down her cheek and felt Terry's left hand, brush against her own. Something stirred inside of her. She glanced around at the girl by his side, before subtly moving her hand away from his touch.

When the band came out, they played 'Last Night on Earth' as Mitch and Troy danced the first dance. Dawn perched on her chair watching them; Mia and Jake ran over and wrapped their arms around her. Jamie sat to her right with her husband Mark and leant close to her mum's ear.

"So, where's your fancy man at, Mum?"

"What fancy man?"

"Mitch tells me you and this journalist have got quite a thing."

"Well, Mitch is wrong, Terry and I are just friends."

"Is he here?"

"Yes, he's over there with his girlfriend."

"Oh. Mum, I'm sorry."

She leant her head against her daughters' as they watched the kids dancing around their feet.

Matt sat down across to them.

"Matt, Joanne, how are you?"

"We're good, Mum. How are you?"

"I'm good. Where's Lucas?"

"At the cake stand with Jake. Where else would he be?" They nodded at each other knowingly.

As she looked around the table at her young adults, parents of their own kids, she felt a warm glow of pride. She'd come through the other side still in one piece and they were all amazing in their own ways.

Troy and Mitch swung each other around the dance floor laughing; Jamie rested her head on her mother's shoulder.

"Look at them, Mum. Who'd have thought our Troy would finally settle down?"

She turned and looked at her daughter, planting a kiss on her head. "I know. For a while there, I wondered if he'd ever learn to be a part of society," she murmured.

She turned back around, catching Terry's eye. She felt her breath catch in her sternum; he was watching her.

Moments later, Michael and Lesley approached. They made an effort to go around the table to each one of them, making conversation and asking about what was going on in their lives. Dawn watched, thinking how sweet it was that they were making sure no-one felt excluded. Every now and then, her eyes would involuntarily flicker through the fairy lights and hanging leaves, towards Terry's seat. Where he and the brunette, who she now knew to be named Katie, were deep in conversation. He was lent forwards, elbows on knees, his eyes intense, body strong. He was interested in whatever she was saying, she realised, maybe even endeared by her words. And Dawn felt a pang of resentment.

Deep down she was hoping they would soon leave so that she could relax without feeling this annoyance at him being there.

"Wow, what a beautiful dress. Is it one of yours?" Lesley asked, placing a glass of champagne into Dawn's hand.

"Bec and Bridge. But thank you, Lesley."

"Well, you always know just how to wear them," she said, sipping at her own champagne. Dawn gave her a genuine smile, and they kissed each other's cheeks.

"It's good to see you," she said genuinely.

She was glad that Michael had found happiness with such a genuine, kind woman, and she found herself watching how they interacted with her kids and grandkids with a sense of fulfilment.

"May I have this dance?" A voice came from the darkness behind her.

She heard a sharp intake of breath from Jamie by her side and she smiled to herself, feeling the meal she'd eaten heavy on her stomach. Instinctively, her eyes shot up to Terry's seat. It was empty. When she looked around, there he was, standing right behind her, with his piercing grey eyes, stubbly square jaw and greying sideburns.

She felt an unexpected anger raging inside of her. *The cheek*. She looked at him, then rose, the whole time holding his gaze, unwavering, her teeth clenched as though to stop herself from reacting. His head furrowed in confusion.

"Doesn't Katie mind?" she asked sharply, nodding towards the approaching woman. He put his arm around Katie's shoulder and laughed, they side-eyed each other.

Dawn's legs wobbled; her sight blurred.

He faced Katie. "Don't mind if your old dad has a dance with this beautiful woman, do you, Katie?" he asked, and when she smiled, Dawn saw how familiar the girl looked. It was Terry's eyes she had.

"Dawn Lewis," she exclaimed. "I'm so happy to finally be introduced. It's only taken him all day."

He chucked Katie's chin.

Dawn took a second to regain herself then shook the girl's hand before being led to the dance floor. Terry swung her around and she rested her head against his chest inhaling the smell of him. She swayed along to the music, looking up at him.

"Finally." He sighed. "I thought you'd been avoiding me all day."

She looked embarrassed.

"What is it?" he asked, pausing to look at her.

"Nothing, I thought Katie… I thought… you know what? It doesn't matter what I thought. I just didn't know you had a daughter."

Realisation dawned on his face. "Oh, Dawny. Oh god, I'm so sorry, I should have introduced you both properly this morning." He smacked his hand against his forehead, with a look of exasperation. "You thought we were together?" He laughed and kissed her head. "What kind of a pervert do you think I am? She's only bloody twenty-four."

She laughed. "Well, I'm fourteen years older than you, so what does that make me?"

"I think it makes you a cougar." He laughed.

"Classy."

He laughed. "I'm just kidding. That's not so bad and besides, you're way younger than most of the women my age."

The song changed, something with more of a beat by Kasabian. The crowd jumped around.

She looked at him. "Want to grab a drink?" she asked. He nodded and followed her to the bar. They ordered a couple of bottles of beer and stood chatting.

The band began to sing 'Against all Odds' and her stomach swirled. They ascended the dance floor alongside Mitch and Troy, and Jamie and Mark, and a few other couples she didn't know. She leant her head against his chest as they swayed along to the music.

She looked at him as a thought struck her. "Hey, so if Katie is twenty-four, that means you already had her when we met in Paris?"

He looked down at her, their faces close, and she rested her head back as he began to talk.

"Apparently so. But I didn't know about her then."

She felt his chest enlarge, then deflate, she felt the vibrations of his voice as it reverberated.

"My previous girlfriend, Jodie, dumped me towards the end of our third year at university, and she just... disappeared off the face of the earth. I was told she'd gone away to do her master's degree and she had, but apparently it was because she found out she was pregnant. Her parents said they'd help out with the baby and get her into a good Uni, if she just got rid of me. She did, and six years later she called me, said she was working for *The Guardian* and didn't want to leave Manchester. I asked why she felt the need to, and she said because her parents decided enough was enough, they wanted her to act like a mother. I was confused – I asked her, 'you have a baby?' She just casually said, 'well, a child. We have a child, and it's time for us to take care of our daughter.' Our daughter, who lived with her parents all of her life in Northampton without my knowing. I was devastated," he said exacerbated.

"I went and met Katie for the first time about a week after that conversation. Her parents took some convincing, but I bought a house in Kettering. I showed them how responsible I was and eventually they allowed me custody, so long as they got her on weekends. I kept my job by commuting to London three days a week and worked from home two; I made changes I'd never dreamed of so that I could be a father."

Dawn leant back and took a deep swig from her bottle.

She didn't know if it was his words or the music, but her eyes were beginning to blur over.

He looked into her eyes then. "It's all a bit of a con, if you ask me."

"The whole custody thing, you mean?" she asked, nibbling at the inside of her lip.

"Nah, not that. I was told single dads were attractive to women… but apparently it only works when they're babies. I nearly gave her back." He grinned.

She looked at him with an open mouth and he laughed.

"You did not," she said, smacking him playfully.

"I'm kidding," he said, grinning and ducking away from her slap.

"So, her mum wasn't the woman you married?"

He grinned. "How did you know I was married?"

"You're down as divorced, seven years, on some silly eligible bachelors list."

He rubbed his chin, still grinning. "Yeah, I met Ronnie on the tube, funnily enough, in 2013. We were married the spring of 2014 and divorced by Christmas. It was all a bit of a farse." He laughed.

"Oh. So has Katie's mum stayed in touch?"

"No, and as far as I know she'd moved to Brazil with her latest boyfriend. She has no interest in being a mum. But her parents have always played a big role in Katie's upbringing. And my parents have loved having a granddaughter, too. I sometimes think they love her more than they ever loved me."

"Well, I don't blame them. She's way cuter." She laughed.

"Eh? I expect that from my family but not you," he

gasped. "But what can I say, she's actually the best thing that ever happened to me."

"That's very sweet," she replied.

"So, the dad card does work. Alright," he whispered, and she poked him. He tipped her chin and locked eyes with her. "But I do like that you got jealous, Lewis."

She smirked at him. "I did not get jealous."

"Well, it certainly looked that way to me."

"You know, I'm sure you weren't this cocky in Paris."

"That's because I knew I didn't have a chance with you back then, you barely even saw me."

"I saw you," she said, her brow creasing.

They swayed along to the band. She looked at him, thinking how handsome he was.

"Hang on. So now you think you do have a chance, eh?"

He turned to face her. "Well, I don't like to be cocky… But yeah… I'm kind of George Clooney these days, you have to admit."

She laughed and leant in, touching his lips with her own.

"You agree then," he said into her lips, and she nipped at the skin of his mouth.

"Ouch. That was mean." He placed the back of his hand against his lip as though looking for blood.

"Aww, you poor thing," she said, sarcastically kissing it better. He took a swig of beer, wrapping the other arm around her waist and swaying her to 'Time of Your Life'.

"The picture I took, that you liked, of you and Jane on the boat…" he stuttered, and her body tensed.

"Yes?" she asked nervously.

"I had it put on a canvas for you a while ago, I wanted to send it to you." Despite the fact that it was Dawn looking at Jane the way he wished she'd look at him, it was too beautiful a moment not to capture. "I thought you might want it, in her memory."

She took a moment to swallow the lump that had formed in the back of her throat. "Wow," she breathed. "You really do understand me."

"I was there, remember? She made you happy, Dawn."

Dawn was stunned by his generosity and understanding. She hadn't noticed most of the dance floor returning to their seats, or her kids grouping together, giggling at their mum and this hunk of a man.

"She came to me, you know, in Paris," he said.

"She came to you?"

He stroked her hair softly, rhythmically. "Yeah, it was after the fitting. On the second night, after I saw something pass between the two of you. She told me that I ought to tell you how I felt. Said I could make you happy. I really looked at her then, and I saw fear. She wanted you to be happy, and she was scared that it wouldn't be with her." He paused a moment to let that sink in. Dawn swallowed the lump forming in her throat. "I told her I wasn't actually interested, that I'd charm anyone to get a good story. I watched the disdain on her face, and I hated it, I hated that I'd lied about you like that." She felt him gulp. "I didn't want to get in the way of your happiness. I didn't want to be your second choice, have you wondering if you'd have been happier with her."

"Do you think that's why she didn't like you?"

"Not in the beginning, but definitely towards the end."

"Are you sure it was a lie?" she quipped, hiding the fear deep inside.

"Obviously I was lying, Dawn. I could see how much you loved each other. You liked me, I knew that, but I wasn't your number one. She was. But Dawn, I know something else, Jane wanted you to be happy and she wouldn't have wanted you to be alone forever. I know how you felt about her."

"You're right," she sighed and looked up at the starry sky, her hips swaying along to the Kacey and Jojo song.

"I came back to Paris," it was a whisper, barely audible. He peered down at her, inquisitively, his chin bunching. "It was almost two years ago now," she said.

"To fashion week?" he asked.

"No, I was done with that. I had this memory of Paris that seemed too good to be true. I wanted to see if it was real. I suppose, I was hoping it would give me that final piece of closure, being with my memories of us."

"And did it?"

"In some sense, yes. But it wasn't the same. It had lost something along the way. I thought it was because I'd grown older or because the city had got poorer, but it wasn't that at all. I know that now. Because I'm not even in the capital, and standing here with you, I feel as though Paris got back its va-va-voom."

He smiled and swept back a loose hair that hung over her eye.

"Va-va-voom," he whispered with a smile, placing his hands on each side of her chin. "Is it weird that that makes sense to me?"

Dawn looked at him and shrugged. Her lips curved into a smile, she lifted onto her toes, and he moved his face slowly towards hers. She pressed her lips against his, he parted his own very slightly. She was stunned by how natural it felt and she allowed her body to melt into his. She backed off, keeping her face close to his, breathing in his breath. It felt as though she had just tasted a drop of water after a long drought.

She held herself back, then on hearing a whoop, glanced around. As she guessed, her family was all watching, whooping, the excitement palpable. Terry's eyes followed hers, and they both turned back to each other and laughed.

"For goodness' sake." She laughed.

Milton Keynes UK
Ingram Content Group UK Ltd.
UKHW022329161223
434422UK00006B/7

9 781805 142768